Enid Blyton

Mr Pink-Whistle Stories

...and other stories

D0528714

Bounty
Books

Published in 2014 by Bounty Books,
a division of Octopus Publishing Group Ltd,
Carmelite House
50 Victoria Embankment
London EC4Y 0DZ
www.octopusbooks.co.uk

An Hachette UK Company
www.hachette.co.uk
Enid Blyton ® Text copyright © 2014 Hodder & Stoughton Ltd.
Illustrations copyright © 2014 Octopus Publishing Group Ltd.
Layout copyright © 2014 Octopus Publishing Group Ltd.

Illustrated by Lesley Smith.

ISBN: 978-0-75372-656-3

A CIP catalogue record for this book is available from the
British Library.

Printed and bound by CPI Group (UK) Ltd, Croydon, CR0 4YY

3 5 7 9 10 8 6 4

CONTENTS

Mr Pink-Whistle Knows How to Bark!

One Wednesday morning Mr Pink-Whistle was walking down Mulberry Lane, watching the children running home from school. They smiled at the plump little man as they passed, and one or two of them whispered among themselves:

"Isn't he like Mr Pink-Whistle – the little man we sometimes read about in our books? But he can't be, of course."

Mr Pink-Whistle sat down on a seat to wait for his bus. All the children seemed to have gone now. But no – here was another one, the last of all.

"A little girl," thought Mr Pink-Whistle. "She doesn't look very happy. Perhaps she was kept in for being naughty."

5

The girl came up and Pink-Whistle saw that she looked frightened. He was just about to speak to her when she darted into a gateway and disappeared.

"Well, I suppose she lives there," said Pink-Whistle to himself. "Hello – who are these, peeping round that corner?"

He saw three boys peering round the corner of the street, some way along. What did they want? He watched them, but they didn't come any further. Soon they drew back and he couldn't see them. He looked round to see if the little girl was anywhere about, and there she was, peering round the gatepost nearby, looking more scared than ever.

"Hello, little girl!" said Pink-Whistle, in his kindly voice. "Are you looking for someone?"

The girl didn't move. She stood behind the gatepost and stared at Mr Pink-Whistle. "Yes," she said. "Well, I'm not exactly looking for someone – I'm looking out for them."

"Oh – someone you don't want to meet?" asked Pink-Whistle. "Who?"

"Well, it's three big boys," said the girl. "You see, my brother is captain of the football eleven at school and he won't have these three boys in the team because they're no good. So they lie in wait for me, and scare me dreadfully."

Pink-Whistle looked down the road to the corner. He saw three heads peeping round again! Oho! So that was why those boys were there, was it – lying in wait for a frightened little girl! The big cowardly bullies!

"What do they do? Do they chase you?" he asked.

"Oh yes and they trip me up; look what they did to my knee yesterday," said the girl, showing him a bandaged knee. "And they pull my hair and throw my hat over the hedge and take my schoolbag away. All because my brother won't have them in his team!"

"Why don't you tell him?" asked Pink-Whistle, sorry for the scared little thing.

"Well, you see, my brother's very brave, and he would fight the three of them," explained the girl. "But they would knock him down and hurt him and maybe he wouldn't be able to play in the match on Saturday. It's a very important match, you know. I might tell him about the boys next week when the match is over."

"I think you must be a very nice sister to have," said Mr Pink-Whistle. "Would you like me to chase those boys away?"

"I don't think you'd have much chance against them," said the girl, still behind the gatepost. "You're not very big, are you, and they're all strong – one's fifteen and as tall as my daddy."

8

"Well, perhaps we could think of something else," said Mr Pink-Whistle. "I can see them peeping round that corner again, looking for you. Now let me see – yes, I've got it! How would you like a very fierce dog to protect you and to chase those boys?"

The little girl looked astonished. "Well, I don't think I like fierce dogs," she said. "And I'm afraid my daddy wouldn't let me keep one."

"Listen," said Mr Pink-Whistle, "I'll lend you a dog to see you home. He shall be yours for a few minutes, see? He can trot down the road beside you and if those boys go for you, he'll go for them, and give them such a fright! You must

shout to warn them, of course: Mind my
dog – he's dangerous!"

"But you haven't a dog with you!" said
the little girl, puzzled.

"Oh, I can soon get him here," said
Pink-Whistle, standing up. "Now, listen,
you pop back into that gateway and hide
under a bush for a minute. When you
hear a dog bark, come along out."

"All right," cried the child, still
astonished. She ran back into the drive
and hid under a bush, waiting. Pink-
Whistle chuckled to himself. "I'm going
to enjoy this!" he said.

Well, Mr Pink-Whistle can do all kinds
of things. He can make himself invisible
and he can even change his shape, for
he is half a brownie. First of all he
muttered a few words that made him
invisible. He disappeared completely –
one moment he was there, the next he
was not! Then he muttered a few more
words, and suddenly, a big dog stood in
his place – a large brown and white one,
with eyes rather like Pink-Whistle's, a
long tail and great big teeth.

He barked, a nice gentle bark because he didn't want to frighten the little girl. She came to the gatepost at once and stared at him. He scampered over to her and licked her hand gently, wagging his great tail. Really, whoever would have thought that Pink-Whistle could bark and wag a tail! He was enjoying himself!

11

"Oh – are you that little man's dog?" asked the girl, and patted him gently. He certainly was big, but he had such nice eyes that she couldn't help liking him. Besides, she loved dogs. "Where's your master gone?" she asked. "He was here a minute ago."

"Woof," said the dog and licked her again. Then he tugged at her skirt as if to say, "Come along. You're safe with me!"

"I'll go home now," said the child. "But please, if those boys rush at me and knock me over, will you bark loudly, dog?"

"WOOF, WOOF!" said Pink-Whistle, and was delighted to find he could bark so loudly! The little girl looked quite startled.

They set out down the road together, Pink-Whistle keeping a little way behind, pattering along on his four paws, pleased to find how easy it was to run like that.

He saw a boy's head pop round the corner and then immediately go back again. So those boys were still there, then, waiting. The little girl didn't see the head pop round because she was

12

watching the big dog and looking round to see if she could see the kind little man who had spoken to her.

She came to the corner and at once the three boys pounced! She gave a scream as one caught her arm.

But listen! "WOOF! WOOOOOOF! WOOOOOOOOF!"

Good gracious, what a bark that was! The boys stopped and stared in fright at the big dog racing round them, barking so loudly.

"Go home!" shouted one boy. Pink-Whistle gave a wonderful snarl and showed all his big doggy teeth. The boy didn't like them at all!

"Leave my dog alone – don't you dare hit him!" cried the little girl as she saw one boy breaking a branch off a nearby tree. "He'll go for you!"

And that is just what Pink-Whistle did! Woofing at the top of his voice, he chased those boys all the way down the street. When one fell down, he leaped on top of him, pretending he was going to bite him! The boy screamed, just as the little girl had so often screamed when she had been chased and knocked down!

How Pink-Whistle enjoyed being a dog chasing those three unkind boys! He went after first one and then another, barking all the time, pretending to nip their ankles as he went. The little girl was half scared and half amused. What a dog! What a kind, brave dog! How she wished he was really hers!

"Hey! You call off this dog of yours and we'll never come near you again!"

shouted one of the boys who had fallen
down, and was trying to push the dog
off him. "Call him off! Go on – we're
scared stiff! I tell you, we'll never come
near you again. We didn't know you had
a dog like this!"

"All right, I'll call him off. But mind, if
you dare even to pull my hair, I'll bring
my dog along again," said the little girl,
fiercely. Then she called to the dog:

"Come here! Come to heel! You can
leave those boys alone now – don't eat
them up this time!"

The dog left the boys and came
running up to the little girl. At once the
three young bullies took to their heels
and fled at top speed. Never, never, never
would they lie in wait for that girl again!

She patted the dog gently. "Come with
me to the butcher's and I'll buy you a
bone," she said. "And when you go back
to that kind little man, tell him I thank
him very, very much for lending you
to me!"

Pink-Whistle trotted off on his four
paws with the little girl, pleased and

proud. What an exciting thing to be a dog for a while!

The little girl bought him a bone, patted him, and away went Pink-Whistle holding it in his mouth exactly as any other dog would! He dropped it at the feet of a hungry-looking terrier he met, and then went into a corner to change back to himself again.

It didn't take long! A few muttered words and the dog disappeared bit by bit, much to the surprise of a cat who was sitting on a nearby wall.

At last Pink-Whistle stood there quite himself again, smiling all over his face. "That was a real adventure!" he said. "Now I must catch that bus, go home to my tea, and tell Sooty my cat what happened to me this afternoon."

Sooty was glad to see his master. "You're very late for your tea," he said. "The hot toast is almost dry."

"Well," said Mr Pink-Whistle, "what do you think I did this afternoon, Sooty? I changed myself into a dog! You should have heard me bark. Just like this – WOOF! WOOOOF! WOOOOOOOOOF!"

Good gracious! What a fright for Sooty! He shot out of the window at the very first woof and he didn't come back till it was dark. Poor Sooty! He had never heard Mr Pink-Whistle bark before – and he hopes he never will again!

Josie, Click and Bun
Give a Party

Josie the curly-haired doll, Bun the toy
bunny and Click the clockwork mouse
were going to give a party. It had been
very cold, dull weather, there was nothing
to do, and Bun and Click were getting
rather naughty. So Josie thought it would
be a good idea to give a party.

"We'll have a very nice time," she said
to Bun and Click. "I'll make some lovely
cakes, and you two can make some pretty
decorations for the rooms. I'll get out
the balloons and you can blow them up."

Well, they sent out cards to Jinky the
elf, Frisky the squirrel, Pippy the pixie,
and to Bun's cousin, Miss Flop-Ears.
They all lived in the next village and they
said they would come on the four
o'clock bus.

"I've made some lovely sandwiches," said Josie when the great day came. "And I've made a cake with candles on it. There are chocolate-iced buns with your names on. And look at the sweets I've made!"

"You're very, very clever, Josie," said Bun. "We shall have a lovely time. Will you tie my bow for me, ready for the party? I can't make it look nice."

Well, Josie tied his new red bow, and she tied Click's yellow one, and then she put on her party dress. It was very frilly and looked pretty. Everything looked nice – the table set with plenty of lovely things to eat, the crackers beside each plate, the balloons hanging around the little room, and the decorations that Bun and Click had made.

"I do feel so happy!" squealed Click, tearing round the room. "Josie, wind me up, will you? I've run round such a lot that I'm almost run down."

Well, you would think that everything was happy and merry and just right, wouldn't you. But it wasn't, because

nobody came at four o'clock! There was
Josie at the door, ready to welcome
everybody – and nobody arrived!

21

"What's happened?" she wondered, looking out of the door. "Certainly there is snow on the ground but that wouldn't stop the others from catching the bus – and we've swept a path right to our front gate."

"They don't like us. They don't want to come," said Bun, suddenly getting gloomy.

"I shall go and see if they are coming down the road," said Click, and before the others could stop him he shot down the path and out into the snowy road.

"Click! Come back! You know you always get stuck in the snow," Josie called crossly. But Click was on his way down the road to the bus-stop.

And of course he did get stuck in the snow! He ran straight into a very deep bit and there he stopped. "Help! I'm stuck! Help me, Josie!" he squealed.

Josie slipped on her coat and ran out. Bun followed her. It took quite a time to find Click because he had gone even deeper into the snow and his squeals could no longer be heard.

Bun found him quite by accident. He trod on him! "Here he is!" he cried, and began to dig him out. Click was crying because Bun had trodden so hard on him.

"Well, it serves you right," said Josie. "You know I don't like you to run out into the snow, Click. Now stop crying and come back. Perhaps our guests will come on the next bus."

"Oh yes," said Bun, cheering up. "Of course they will. A-TISH-oo!"

"There! Bun has caught cold coming out into the snow to help you," said Josie, vexed. "Bun, do you feel as if you've got a cold already?"

"Yes. A-tish-OO!" said Bun. "I'm afraid I have. But please don't make me go to bed before the party, Josie."

They went back indoors, Click was still crying, Bun sneezing and Josie scolding. And what a shock they got when they went indoors! The sandwiches were gone. The cakes were gone. The balloons had disappeared and so had the crackers.

And the lovely big cake with candles was gone too. Josie looked at the table in horror.

"Who's been here? Somebody's been in and stolen our goodies while we were out in the road. We've got nothing for our guests to eat when they come!"

"It's all my fault," wailed Click. "If I hadn't run out this wouldn't have happened."

"A-tish-oooooooo," said Bun, dismally.

Josie nearly cried. "Oh dear, oh dear; here's all our tea stolen, Bun with a cold, and four guests coming on the next bus."

"Who could have stolen everything?" said Bun, looking round. "Oooh, I say – what's that?"

He pointed with his paw at a black heap in front of the fire. Josie stared. Click gave a scream and backed into the corner.

"It's a cat!" he squealed. "A big black cat. Chase him away before he eats me."

"He must be the thief," said Bun, not stopping to think that a cat wouldn't eat crackers and balloons. "He's had all the cakes and sandwiches. Wicked cat! Shoo!"

The cat untucked its head and looked at the angry rabbit out of bright-green eyes. "I lost my way in the snow," he said. "I came in for shelter and warmth."

"You're a bad, wicked cat," said Josie, and she took up her broom. "Go away! Shoo!"

She swept the cat into a corner. It put out its claws and spat. It simply wouldn't be swept out of the house. It went and sat down by the fire again, its green eyes gleaming brightly.

Bun opened a cupboard door. He

nodded at Josie and she suddenly swept the yowling cat into the cupboard. Bun slammed the door and locked it. Aha! The cat was caught.

"Now, if we can find out who the cat belongs to we can tell all about his greediness and make his owner pay for the damage," said Josie. "I never heard of such a thing! A cat walking into a house like that and eating absolutely everything."

"Except the cream and the milk," said Click, peeping into the jugs. "What a strange cat! Did he eat the balloons too, do you think?"

The cat began to make a tremendous noise in the cupboard. He yowled and miaowed and spat and clawed at the door.

"He's gone mad," said Bun. "A-tish-oooo!"

"Oh dear. Get a clean hanky, Bun," said Josie. "You really ought to go to bed. Whatever are we to do with all those guests coming and no party?"

Then they all jumped dreadfully, because a voice spoke out of the air:

27

"What have you done with my cat?"

Josie, Click and Bun stared all round the room. Who was speaking? There was nobody there but themselves! Click ran under the table in a fright. Bun took hold of Josie's hand. He was trembling.

"Who's speaking?" he said to Josie. "I can't see anyone."

"What have you done with my cat?" said the voice again – and then someone began to appear in the room, bit by bit; first his feet, then his legs, then his middle, then his hands and arms, and last of all his head!

And who do you suppose it was? Can you guess? It was old Mr Pink-Whistle, that kind little man, half human, half brownie, who goes about the world to see what wrong things he can put right!

But how angry he looked now! He pointed to the cupboard. "You've shut my cat in there. You are unkind and cruel. He came out for a walk with me and got lost in the snow. You might have let him wait here in the warm till I came."

28

Josie stared at Mr Pink-Whistle as if she couldn't believe her eyes. Then she ran to him. "I know who you are! I've often read stories about you. You're Mr Pink-Whistle, dear kind Pink-Whistle! Oh, I didn't know it was *your* cat!"

Bun went to the door of the cupboard and opened it. Out sprang the black cat at once. Mr Pink-Whistle bent down to stroke him.

"Poor old Sooty! Why did they treat you like that then?"

Josie explained, going rather red. "We went out for a few minutes and left the door open. And when we came back all our nice goodies were gone – and as Sooty was here we thought he'd had them. I'm so sorry!"

"I know who took them," said Mr Pink-Whistle at once. "I met the red goblins down the road, and they were carrying cakes and balloons and sandwiches. I thought it was very peculiar. Well, they must have eaten them all by now, I'm afraid."

"And we've got guests coming to our party by the next bus!" said Josie in despair.

"I can do something about that," said Mr Pink-Whistle, feeling very cheerful because he had happened on something he could put right. "Just go and look in

that cupboard you put Sooty in."

And, will you believe it, the shelves were full of cakes and jellies and trifles and biscuits! And there was a little pile of balloons all waiting to be blown up.

Well, well, well! Click squealed in delight. Josie kissed Mr Pink-Whistle, and Bun actually patted the cat. Then he sneezed loudly.

"Bun! Go to bed at once!" said Josie. "You will be very ill if you don't!"

"Poor Bun!" said Mr Pink-Whistle,

kindly. "Here, sniff this – it will soon put you right."

He held out a tiny little bottle filled with red liquid. Bun put his nose to it and sniffed. Then he sneezed seventeen times without stopping. When at last he stopped he looked at Josie. "Sneezed my cold all away!" he said. "Not a bit of it left. Thank you very much, Mr Pink-Whistle."

"Well, you have brought us good luck," said Josie, pleased. "Oh, look – there's a robin at the windowsill with a note in its beak."

The note made them all very sad again. "Listen to this," said Josie. "'Dear Josie, Click and Bun: The snow is so thick in our village that the buses aren't running. So we can't come to your party. We are very, very sorry. Love from Jinky, Pippy, Frisky and Flop-Ears.'"

"Oh dear!" said Josie, almost in tears. "We've got a whole lot of lovely things to eat again, and Bun's cold made better – and now our guests aren't coming. What a dreadful disappointment."

"Well," said Mr Pink-Whistle, "I could send Sooty to fetch three other guests if you like. And if you'd have me and Sooty for guests, too, we could make a very nice party."

"Oh yes," said Josie, pleased. "Do send Sooty for some more guests. They are sure to be nice if they are friends of yours."

So off went Sooty through the snow – and do you know who he brought back with him? He brought Silky, Moonface and the old Saucepan Man! Josie cried out in delight.

"Oh, I've always wanted to meet you! Oh, what a really lovely party!"

"Hearty?" said the old Saucepan Man, mishearing as usual. "Yes, I'm hale and hearty, thank you. Awfully nice of you to ask us out to tea. I've dressed myself up in my very best kettles and saucepans for you!"

Well, they all had a wonderful time. The tea was soon eaten, and because there were not quite enough jellies, Josie was sent to the cupboard again – and there on the shelf were two more. How marvellous.

Mr Pink-Whistle enjoyed himself more than anyone, especially when he was the blind man in blind-man's-buff and caught the old Saucepan Man. He couldn't think what he was, and when Josie asked him the name of the person he had caught he said, "I must have caught the kitchen stove," and Click laughed so much that he jerked his key out.

Everyone was given a balloon. Even Sooty had one – he said it was the first balloon he had ever had. Click wasn't a

bit afraid of him when he said goodbye, and shook paws as if he were Sooty's very best friend!

"Thank you for your lovely party, Josie" said Mr Pink-Whistle.

"Oh, Mr Pink-Whistle, it wasn't my party – it was yours!" cried Josie. "Thank *you*, Mr Pink-Whistle. You are every bit as nice as you are in your stories."

So he is. You'll find that out when you meet him!

Mr Pink-Whistle
Comes Along

"Sooty!" called Mr Pink-Whistle to his big black cat. "I'm going for a walk. It's a lovely sunny winter's day. I'll be back in time for lunch."

Sooty went to the door to see him off. He went briskly down the garden path and out of the gate. The frost crunched under his feet as he went, and the pale December sun shone down on him. What a lovely day!

"I think I'll go down to the pond to see if there are any children sliding on the ice," he thought. So off he went, down the lane, up the hill, down the hill, and across a meadow where frost whitened the long grass in the ditches.

Mr Pink-Whistle was just putting his leg over the stile to go to the pond when his sharp ears heard a sound. He had pointed brownie ears and could hear like a hare!

"Now, what's that?" he thought, a leg half over the stile. "Is it an animal? Or a child? Or just a noise?"

It seemed to come from a little tumble-down shed by the hedge. Mr Pink-Whistle listened. Yes, there certainly was a noise – a sniffy sort of noise: Sniff-sniff-gulp, sniff-sniff!"

"I'd better go and find out," said Pink-Whistle, and he got down from the stile and went to the little shed. He poked his

head inside. It was rather dark and he couldn't see anything at first. Then he saw something white. "Dear me!" said Pink-Whistle. "Is that a face I see? Does it belong to someone? Who are you?"

The face was peeping out of a pile of hay in the corner of the shed.

"Yes, but please go away. This is my shed. It's private."

Pink-Whistle didn't go away. He was sure that he could see that face was very miserable. He came right into the shed.

Somebody scrambled out of the hay crossly. It was a boy of about ten. "I told you this was *my* shed," he said. "It's on my father's land and he said I could have it for my own. You're trespassing!"

"Was it you I heard sniff-sniff-sniffing?" asked Pink-Whistle. "What's the matter?"

"Nothing," said the boy. "Nothing to do with you anyway. Don't you know when people want to be alone? I wish you'd get out of my shed."

"I'm going," said Pink-Whistle. "But it's a pity you haven't even a dog to keep you company. If you're unhappy, it's nice to have a dog's nose on the knee."

He walked back to the door. "Come back," said the boy suddenly, sitting down on the hay and rubbing a very dirty hand over his face. "I like what you said just now. You might understand if I tell you something. You wouldn't have said that if you hadn't understood what friends dogs are, would you?"

"No," said Pink-Whistle, turning back. "So it's something to do with a dog, is it? Your own dog, I suppose."

"Yes, said the boy in a shaky sort of voice. "You see, I've got no brothers or sisters, so my dad gave me a dog for my own. My very own, you understand – not one that's shared by the whole family. Buddy was my own, every whisker of him, every hair."

"That's a splendid thing," said Pink-Whistle. "I expect you belonged to him as much as he belonged to you. You were his friend as much as he was yours."

"I'm glad you understand," said the boy. "It's nice to tell somebody. Well, Buddy's gone. Somebody's stolen him. He was a black spaniel with big, loving eyes, and he cost my father a lot of money. That's why he's been stolen, because he's valuable."

Sniff-sniff-sniff! The boy rubbed his hand over his eyes again. "I'm ten," he said, ashamed, "and too old to make a fuss like this, like a four-year-old. I know all that, so you needn't tell me. But a dog sort of gets right into your heart if he's your own."

"I shall begin to sniff, too, in a minute,"

said Pink-Whistle. "I know exactly what you feel. You're thinking how miserable your dog will be without you, and you're hoping that nobody is being cruel to him, and you're wondering if he's cowering down in some corner, puzzled and frightened. Well, that's enough to make anyone feel miserable."

"He disappeared yesterday," said the boy. "Two men came to the farm to ask if they could buy chickens – and I'm sure they took Buddy away. They may have

given him some meat with a sleeping powder in it and got him like that. The police say they can't trace the men and they haven't had any report of a black spaniel anywhere."

"I see," said Pink-Whistle. "Er – do you happen to know me by any chance, young lad?"

"My name's Robin," said the boy. "No, I don't know you. I've never ever seen you before, have I?"

He peered closely at Pink-Whistle. The sun shone in at the little shed window just then and he suddenly saw Pink-Whistle clearly. He saw his green eyes and pointed ears and he gave a little cry.

"Wait! Wait! Yes, I've seen your picture somewhere in a magazine or a book. Yes, I remember now. Why – surely you're not Mr Pink-Whistle?"

"I am," said Pink-Whistle, beaming all over his face, pleased that the boy knew him. "And I like to go about the world putting wrong things right."

"Get back Buddy for me then, please, please, please!" said Robin, clutching

hold of Mr Pink-Whistle's arm. "I never thought you were real, but you are. Can you get back Buddy?"

"I'll do my best," said Pink-Whistle. "I'll go now. Cheer up, get out of this dark shed and go home and find some work to do. Perhaps I can put things right for you."

He walked out of the shed. Robin ran after him, suddenly very cheerful indeed. He was amazed. To think that Mr Pink-Whistle should come along just then – what a wonderful thing!

Pink-Whistle went back home. He called Sooty, his cat, and told her about Robin. "Go to the farm and speak to the farm cats," he said. "They will have

noticed these two men and have seen if Buddy was taken away by them. Find out all you can."

Sooty ran off, tail in the air. She soon came back with the news. "Yes, Master! The farm cats say that the men came back that evening, threw down meat for Buddy and then went away. Buddy ate it and fell asleep. Then the men came back and put him into a sack. The cats heard them saying they were going to Ringdown Market on Thursday. You will find them there."

"Thank you, Sooty," said Pink-Whistle. "That's all I want to know."

The next Thursday, Pink-Whistle set off to Ringdown Market. It was a long way away, but he got there at last. What a babble of sound there was! Horses whinnying, sheep baaing, hens clucking, ducks quacking, turkeys gobbling, geese hissing and cackling!

Pink-Whistle looked for a black spaniel. There were three for sale at the market. Which was Robin's? Mr Pink-Whistle decided to make himself invisible. This was a gift he sometimes used, and he used it now!

One moment there was a kindly old man walking about – the next moment he wasn't there at all! An old woman selling eggs was most astonished. She blinked her eyes in wonder and then forgot about it. Pink-Whistle went up to a black spaniel. "Buddy!" he whispered. "Buddy!"

The dog took no notice. So that one wasn't Robin's dog. Pink-Whistle went up to the second spaniel and whispered. But he wasn't Robin's dog either.

"Buddy!" whispered Pink-Whistle to

the third spaniel, who was lying miserably on some sacks behind two men selling hens. "Buddy!"

The dog sprang up at once, his tail wagging. He looked all round. Who had called him by his name? One of the men turned round sharply.

"Lie down you!" he shouted. Pink-Whistle felt very angry indeed. Aha! These fellows wanted punishing. They wanted frightening. Well, he would have a grand game and give them a wonderful punishment.

He began to bark like a dog and Buddy pricked up his ears at once. Then Pink-Whistle pretended that Buddy was speaking.

"Hens, peck these men!" he cried. And then it seemed to the men as if a whole flock of invisible hens were all round them, pecking hard – but really, of course, it was Mr Pink-Whistle jabbing at them with his hard little forefinger – peck-peck-peck!

The men cowered back, squealing. Everyone came to see what the matter

was. Pink-Whistle called out again in a barking sort of voice, so that it seemed as if Buddy was talking: "Geese, attack these men!"

And dear me, what a cackling there was from old Pink-Whistle then, what a hissing – and what a jab-jab-jabbing from top to bottom of the scared men. Everyone stared, amazed. What was happening? Where did the cackling and hissing come from? Who was jabbing the men?

"Serves them right," said somebody. "I never did like those two."

And then Pink-Whistle decided to be a butting goat! What fun he was having – and what a wonderful punishment he was giving the two men!

"Goat, butt them!" he cried. The men looked everywhere, scared, wondering if an invisible goat was coming at them.

Biff! Pink-Whistle ran first at one man and then another. *Biff! Bang! Biff!* The men felt exactly as though a big, rather solid goat was butting them back and front. Pink-Whistle butted one man right

over and he rolled on top of Buddy.
Buddy promptly snapped at him and
growled.

Pink-Whistle immediately growled too,
and talking in his growling voice, said:
"Bull, toss these men!"

The men gave a loud howl. Hens had
pecked them, geese had jabbed them, a
goat had butted them! Surely, surely they
were not going to be tossed by a bull,
and an invisible one, too, coming at them
from any side!

"Run for it!" yelled one man, and he
ran for his life. The other followed. Pink-
Whistle galloped after them, making his

feet sound like a bull's hooves – *clippitty-clippitty-clop*. How the men howled!

Pink-Whistle couldn't follow them very far because he was laughing so much. How he laughed! People were really puzzled to hear loud chuckles and not to see anyone there.

"Well, I don't know what's upset those two fellows," said a burly farmer, "but I'm glad to see the back of them. Rascals, both of them!"

Pink-Whistle went back to where the dog Buddy lay on the sacks, puzzled and frightened. Buddy suddenly heard a quiet, kindly voice talking to him, and invisible fingers undid the knot of rope that tied him to a rail.

"Come with me, Buddy," said the voice, and Buddy went obediently. He sniffed at Mr Pink-Whistle's invisible legs. How very peculiar to smell legs that didn't seem to be there! Buddy couldn't understand it – but then, he didn't really understand anything that had happened since he had left Robin. His world seemed quite upside-down and not at all a nice place.

It was a long way to the farm where Robin lived – but as they got nearer to it Buddy became very excited indeed. His nose twitched. He pulled against the hand on his collar.

"Not so fast, Buddy," said Mr Pink-Whistle. "I want to come with you."

Buddy took another sniff at the invisible legs. Well, they smelled all right, so the person with them ought to be all right, too. He trotted along obediently, getting more and more excited.

It was dark when at last they came to the farm. Buddy pulled and pulled at

Pink-Whistle's hand. The little man led him to his kennel. "Get in there and wait!" he ordered. "And bark. Bark loudly!"

Buddy crept in and then he barked. How loudly he barked. "Wuff-wuff-wuff, WUFF-WUFF. Robin, I'm back, where are you? WUFF-WUFF!"

And Robin heard of course. He would know Buddy's bark anywhere! He sprang up at once, his face shining. "Mum! That's Buddy's bark! He's back!" he cried and raced out of the house to the yard. He came to the kennel, calling joyfully:

"Buddy! Buddy! I'm here!"

And, before Buddy could squeeze past the invisible Mr Pink-Whistle, there was Robin, squeezing into the kennel! He got right in, and then you really couldn't tell which was boy and which was dog, they hugged and licked and rolled and patted, and yelped and shouted so joyfully together!

At last, tired out, they sat peacefully together in the kennel; Buddy's nose on Robin's knee and Robin's arm round

Buddy's neck. Only Buddy's tongue was busy, lick-lick-licking at Robin's hand.

"Buddy" I do wish I could say a big thank you to Mr Pink-Whistle!" said Robin. "I don't even know where he lives, though. I'd say, Mr Pink-Whistle, I'm your friend for ever and ever!"

Pink-Whistle heard it all. He was peering in at the kennel, as happy as could be. He had put a lot of things right in his life, but surely this was one of the very best! He stole away in the darkness, a very happy little man indeed.

Mr Pink-Whistle
Gives a Helping Hand

Now, one day two children came knocking at Mr Pink-Whistle's door. They were twins, and as alike as two peas in a pod, one a boy and one a girl.

Mr Pink-Whistle was asleep in his chair, and it was Sooty, his cat, who answered the door.

"Oh! Are you Sooty?" said the boy, in delight. "I've read about you. Please – we've come to see Mr Pink-Whistle. He puts wrong things right, doesn't he?"

"He does," said Sooty. "Come along in. He's resting just now – it's hard work putting so many wrong things right, you know. You sit down. and have a cup of cocoa and a biscuit with me, and tell me what's wrong."

"Well," said the girl, "we live with our

mother. Our father is dead, so Mummy works hard at taking in people's laundry. She grows flowers, too, and sells them in the market."

"Well, what's wrong about that?" said Sooty.

"Nothing," said the boy. "But I'll tell you what is wrong! There's a horrible, spiteful man next door, and he doesn't like us two. We are a bit noisy sometimes, and our ball does go into his garden once or twice a week – but he's unkind to our mother because of us!"

"Dear me – what does he do?" asked Sooty, giving the cocoa to the children.

"He lights a bonfire when the wind is in our direction!" said the boy. "And it kills Mum's flowers and it blackens all the clean washing hanging out on the line!"

"What a horrid thing to do!" said Sooty. "I suppose she has to wash it all over again?"

"Yes. And if she's tired it makes her cry," said the girl. "And she does so love her flowers, and she can't bear to see them all withered and scorched and besides, she can't sell them then."

"And we want to know if Mr Pink-Whistle can put things right for us," said the boy. "He's so kind, isn't he? He could put them right, I know."

"I really don't see how," said Sooty, handing them a tin of biscuits.

"When will he be awake?" asked the girl. "We simply must ask him. We've come a long way."

"I'll go and see if he's awake now," said Sooty, and hurried away to find out.

Mr Pink-Whistle was awake. He was in a tremendous flurry, too, because he had

promised to go out to tea with his friend
Mr Winkle, and here it was almost half
past four now! Goodness, what a hurry
he was in!

"What's happened to my clean
handkerchiefs? Where's my hat-brush?
Where did I put my new shoes?" Pink-
Whistle rushed about from place to place,
muttering all the time.

"Master, there are two children to see
you," began Sooty. "But I am sure you
won't have time."

"Dear dear – no, I'm afraid I shan't,"
said Pink-Whistle, looking at his watch.
"What do they want?"

Sooty told him about the twins and

their mother, and how she took in laundry and grew flowers to sell – and how the man next door spoiled everything by lighting bonfires as soon as the wind was in their direction.

"I told them there was nothing you could do to put it right," said Sooty.

"Nothing I can do! Why, of course there's something," cried Pink-Whistle. "All they want is a little spell to change the direction of the wind when that spiteful fellow lights his bonfire! Now, Sooty, you know where my wind-spells are kept, don't you? In the bottom drawer of my chest. Take one out and give it to the children with my love. It's just a tiny packet of yellow powder, and all they have to do is to blow it into the wind."

"Oh – I didn't think of a wind spell!" said Sooty. "Whatever are you looking for, Master? You've got everything you want, surely?"

"My gloves, Sooty, my gloves!" said Pink-Whistle, pulling out drawer after drawer.

58

"You've got them on, Master," said Sooty, and Pink-Whistle looked at his hands and laughed.

"So I have. Well, I must go. Give my best wishes to the two children, and hand them the wind-spell. Tell them not to use all the powder at once – just a bit at a time, each time the man lights his bonfire. The wind will change, and the thick smoke won't hurt their flowers or the washing on the line. Now, goodbye. Have something nice for my supper, please!"

Out hurried Mr Pink-Whistle, and Sooty tidied up and then went to the bottom drawer of the chest. There he saw some packets of yellow powder – the wind-spells.

He picked out a nice big one and went back to the children.

"Oooh!" they said, when he told them what he was giving them. "How kind of Mr Pink-Whistle! Please thank him. Now we shall be all right!"

They hurried home, very pleased.

"There's not a breath of wind at present," said the girl, "or we might try a bit of the spell and watch the wind blow away in the opposite direction. Never mind – the very next time that horrid man lights his bonfire to spoil Mummy's washing, we'll use it!"

The next day, when the twins were playing with their bows and arrows, an arrow went into the next-door garden. The twins peered through the fence to see where it was. Perhaps they could reach it with a stick. So they poked a stick through the palings – but Mr Grumps saw them at once, and shouted, "Now what are you doing – poking about in my garden? Am I never to have any peace?"

The twins ran indoors frightened. "Oh dear – tomorrow is Mum's washing day," they said. "Old Mr Grumps is sure to light his bonfire because we've annoyed him again. Where's that spell? We may have to use it!"

Well, as soon as the twins' mother hung out her spotless washing the next

morning, Mr Grumps went down to fetch
sticks for his bonfire.

"Oh, please don't light your bonfire
today," begged the twins' mother. "I've
just spent hours doing so much washing
– shirts and sheets, towels and blankets,
dresses and overalls – please, I beg you,
don't light your bonfire!"

"Bah!" said Mr Grumps. "Why don't
you train your children better? Then
maybe I'd train my bonfire not to smoke
on your washing day!"

"You'll spoil my beautiful roses and
delphiniums!" cried the poor woman, as
she saw Mr Grumps sweep up all kinds of
rubbish for his bonfire. "And I want to
take them to the market tomorrow, to
sell at my flower-stall!"

"Hah! They won't be much good for
selling!" said Mr Grumps. "I'll just wait
for the wind to strengthen a bit, then
I'll get my fire going."

Well, in half an hour that bonfire was
going well, and great clouds of black,
evil-smelling smoke began to roll across
the twins' garden. It scorched the tall

delphiniums, it made the roses wilt –
and soon it began to blacken the
washing. But wait – what was this that
the twins were doing?

"Quick! Use the spell before the bonfire
gets worse," said the boy, and he undid
the packet of yellow powder. "Now – both
together – blow the wind-spell into the
wind. Oh, how I hope it works!"

Now Sooty had quite forgotten to tell
the children that only a bit must be used
at a time and they used the whole spell at
once! The yellow powder flew into the

air – and into the wind, of course. Then a strange thing happened!

The spell bent the wind back – it made it change its direction! Instead of blowing all over the twins' garden, it blew back into Mr Grumps's. But it blew back there very fiercely indeed! The wind-spell had changed the strong breeze into quite a gale, which raged round Mr Grumps's garden and tried to get out of it. But it couldn't – the spell kept it there in his garden, blowing round and round.

The bonfire began to blaze as the wind blew strongly into it. The smoke rose high and wide. It blackened Mr Grumps's flowers. It scorched his fine lettuces. It blew into the open windows of his house and filled the rooms with black fog.

And then something else happened. The bonfire flames stretched out hot fingers to Mr Grumps's fine new shed. It burned his favourite spade lying nearby. It began to burn his barrow – and now it was sending flames up the side of his wooden shed!

The twins were amazed when the spell

changed the wind so quickly but they became frightened when they saw what else was happening. Oh – Mr Grumps's lovely new shed! Oh, his nice barrow – and oh, look, his lettuces were all withering!

"Quick – quick – we must do something!" cried the boy, and he ran to get the garden hose. He fitted it on the tap with trembling fingers, and then with a *whoooooosh* the water began to pour from the hose on to the flames!

Mr Grumps rushed out of his house in amazement and dismay. What was this! His bonfire wasn't harming that woman's washing next door – it was burning up his own possessions! Look at his barrow – and his shed would soon be nothing but ashes! Why, oh why had he lit that bonfire to do the people next door a bad turn?

Then he saw what the twins were doing – trying to quench the flames! The girl had filled a bucket of water, too, and was trying to put out the flames round the burning barrow. *Sizzle-sizzle-sizzle*!

At last the bonfire was out and only a wisp of black smoke rose up from it. The shed had been saved, the barrow wasn't too badly burned – but the spade was no use and the lettuces were all gone.

"Oh, you kind children!" cried Mr Grumps. "You've saved my shed. My house might have caught fire, too. Oh, to think I was doing you such a bad turn – and you've done me a good one in return.

I'll never be unkind to you again, never!"

The girl twin began to cry. She had been so frightened and upset. "You were very bad to try to spoil my mother's washing!" she wept. "But we were bad to make the wind blow the other way and nearly burn all your things up. We used a wind-spell, Mr Grumps – and it changed the wind!"

Mr Grumps didn't believe this. He didn't believe in spells or magic or anything like that. He patted the girl on the shoulder.

"Rubbish, my dear!" he said. "It wasn't a wind-spell, you know it wasn't. It was just that the wind suddenly changed, as it sometimes does, and I got the flames and smoke instead of you. But you were kind and good – you tried to save my things for me!"

When the news got round to Mr Pink-Whistle, he was astonished. "Sooty!" he said to his black cat, "Sooty – you must have forgotten to tell those children only to use part of the wind-spell at a time!"

"Yes, I did forget, Master," said Sooty, with a sly smile. "But never mind, old man Grumps and the twins and their mother are now all as friendly as can be – so you've managed to put things right again, just as you always do. You're a wonder, Mr Pink-Whistle – things always go right for you!"

Good old Mr Pink-Whistle – I'd like him for my best friend, wouldn't you?

Mr Pink-Whistle
Is a Conjurer!

Mr Pink-Whistle was going along the road one morning, when he saw a notice tied neatly to a garden gate. He stopped to read it.

A CONJURING SHOW, FULL OF MAGIC AND
MARVEL, WILL BE GIVEN IN OUR GARAGE
TOMORROW AFTERNOON, AT THREE O'CLOCK.
TICKETS: CHILDREN 30P GROWN-UPS 60P.
THE MONEY IS TO GO TO OLD MRS JORDAN,
TO BUY HER A WHEELCHAIR.

"Well, well – I think I'd better attend this conjuring show," said Mr Pink-Whistle. "I know old Mrs Jordan. She used to keep the sweet-shop, and always gave the children a few extra sweets in their bags! Then she broke her leg and couldn't walk, and now people are helping to buy her a wheelchair. Yes – I must certainly go!"

A boy came running to the gate when he saw Mr Pink-Whistle there. "Are you reading my notice?" he said. "Oh, I hope you are coming, sir – we want the garage absolutely full. You see, we want to buy—"

"Yes, I've read all about it," said Pink-Whistle. "I'm very pleased to help. I've known old Mrs Jordan for years. May I ask who the conjurer is going to be?"

"Well – actually I'm doing the conjuring," said the boy. "My name's Derek Fuller, and I had a marvellous conjuring set for Christmas. I've practised and practised, and I know quite a lot of tricks now. Come and see my conjuring set. It's in the garage."

Mr Pink-Whistle went into the garage and saw the conjuring set. "I can make an egg come in an empty bag," said Derek. "And five ribbons out of one ribbon. And I can put four hankies on top of one another, shake them out – and

they'll all suddenly be tied together –
and…"

"You are certainly clever," said Pink-
Whistle, admiringly. "I shall look forward
to tomorrow. May I buy six tickets,
please, as I would like to bring a few
friends. And how much would you charge
for a cat to come?"

"A cat! Well, I hadn't really thought,"
said Derek, surprised. "What about one
penny?"

"Well – say two pence," said Pink-
Whistle. "It's my pet cat I want to bring
– he does so enjoy things of this kind.
Let me see now – that's three pounds

and sixty-two pence. Here you are."

"Oh, thank you," said Derek, and gave him the tickets, made of neatly cut-out bits of paper. "That's the one for the cat – I've marked 2p on it. Three o'clock tomorrow, sir. See you then!"

But Mr Pink-Whistle saw Derek before three o'clock the next day – he saw him when he came back from his walk half an hour later, looking very miserable indeed. He was taking down the notice from the gate. "Hey – what's happened?" said Pink-Whistle, in astonishment. "Is the conjuring show off?"

"Yes, and I'll have to give you your money back," said Derek. "You remember when I took you into the garage to show you my conjuring set? Well, I must have left the doors open and someone came in after I'd gone, and stole my conjuring set! I do feel so terribly upset about it."

"What a very mean trick!" said Pink-Whistle, shocked. "Who was it? Have you any idea?"

"Yes; Tom, the big boy down the street," said Derek. "He's always wanted to borrow my set and I wouldn't lend it to him, because I knew I'd never get it back. I saw him running down the road a few minutes ago with a big red box under his arm – I'm sure he took it."

"Well, never mind. We'll still have the conjuring show. I'm a bit of a conjurer myself you know," said Pink-Whistle. "For instance, I can make myself disappear – like this!"

And lo and behold, he was gone! Absolutely gone! Derek stared in amazement. Then he gave a shout. "Oh! I know

73

who you are! Of course – you're Mr Pink-Whistle, aren't you, the little man who goes about the world putting wrong things right? Of course, of course!"

"Quite right," said Mr Pink-Whistle, appearing again, much to the astonishment of a passing dog. "Well now – I think we could do a marvellous show between us, don't you agree?"

"Oh *yes*!" said Derek, his eyes shining with excitement. "Yes, yes, yes – a thousand yesses! What shall we do?"

"Come into the garage," said Mr Pink-Whistle. "We'll make a few plans."

Well, the two of them disappeared into the garage and shut the doors, and what a lot of exciting plans they made.

"I'm bringing my cat Sooty tomorrow afternoon, as you know," said Pink-Whistle, "and he'll do anything we say. We'll make him perform as well, shall we?"

Derek could hardly sleep that night for excitement. He tossed and turned, thinking of all the tricks and magic he and Mr Pink-Whistle would do the next

day. What fun it was going to be!

The next morning came at last and Derek set out rows of chairs and benches in the garage, and borrowed some big boxes from the greengrocer for the audience to sit on as well. The notice was back on the gate, of course, and Derek was busy selling tickets all morning. Tom, the mean boy from down the road, who had stolen the conjuring set, was most surprised to see that the Show was still going to be given. He stood looking in at the garage, puzzled.

"Ha – come to bring back my conjuring set?" said Derek, spotting him.

"Who says I took it?" said the boy, sullenly. "You and your potty conjuring set! I'll come this afternoon, see if I don't, and spoil your show, for saying I took your set!"

"You'd better not," said Derek, in alarm. He simply couldn't have anything go wrong this afternoon!

At three o'clock the garage was full, and there were quite a lot of children standing at the back. Derek was very pleased to see how many tickets had been sold. He and Mr Pink-Whistle had made a slightly raised platform of planks at the end of the garage, and on it was a table with a black cloth over it, and a silver wand lying across it. On a stool lay the things that Derek was going to use at the show – a top hat borrowed from his father, several hankies, some new-laid eggs and other things.

Mr Pink-Whistle was there, but no one could see him because he had made himself quite invisible. Sooty his cat was

there, too, looking extremely smart with a red bow round his neck and one on his tail. He was very excited.

At three o'clock Derek walked on to the little platform and bowed. His mother had made him a cloak out of an old black velvet curtain, and lined it with red, and he looked very grand. He bowed to the clapping audience.

"Thank you for coming here," he said. "I will now begin my show which, I hope, will help to by old Mrs Jordan a wheelchair. You will see marvellous things this afternoon, magical things that will puzzle you and fill you with wonder. But first I must introduce to you my helper – a black cat. As you know, witches have

77

black cats and I, being a conjurer, must have one, too. Sooty, bow to the audience."

And to everyone's immense astonishment Sooty came on to the little platform and bowed graciously to everyone. They could hardly believe their eyes. A cat bowing! Whatever next?

Well, it turned out to be a perfectly marvellous afternoon. First Derek did the fly-away trick.

"I will show you my fly-away magic," he said. "See, I will put on my father's top hat – and when I tell it to fly away, it will do so! Watch!"

He put on the top hat and waved his wand. "Hat! Fly away!" he cried. And hey presto, the hat rose into the air and flew gracefully all round the stage! When Derek shouted "Come back, hat!" it came back to his head.

Of course, it was really the invisible Mr Pink-Whistle who had taken the hat off Derek's head, and run all round the stage with it, holding it high in his hand, and then popped the hat back on Derek's head. But as nobody could see Pink-Whistle, they thought the hat was flying all by itself!

"Now hat – fly to my little cat-attendant," shouted Derek, and at once the hat shot off his head and went to Sooty. It was far too big for him, of course, and everyone roared to see him trying to get it off his nose!

"Make the hat fly to *my* head!" cried a girl in the front row of the audience. In a flash the hat was off Sooty's head, and flying through the air to the girl's head.

How she screamed for joy at such magic! It was really just Pink-Whistle, of course, taking the hat to her, unseen.

"Wonderful!" shouted the audience. "Do some more tricks, Make the cat do something."

"Sooty – please dance and sing!" commanded Derek, and Sooty at once began to do a comical little dance – and behind him, still invisible, Mr Pink-Whistle sang a wonderful song, each verse ending with "Mee-OW, mee-OW, mee-OW." All the audience joined in of course. How they clapped little Sooty!

"And now I will make anything belonging to you members of the audience disappear into thin air!" cried Derek. "Who will bring up a handkerchief – or a book – or a purse? Don't be afraid, you'll get them all back."

Harry came up with a comic. John came up with a bag of sweets. Beth came with a red hanky. Derek took them all.

"Stand by me," he said. "Now, Beth – throw your hanky into the air, please."

Beth threw it up – and it disappeared!

Yes, it absolutely vanished. No wonder it did, for the unseen Pink-Whistle had neatly caught it and stuffed it into his pocket, where it promptly disappeared. Then Harry threw up his comic and that vanished too. So did John's bag of sweets. It was too mysterious for words!

"I want my sweets back," said John, looking all round. "Where are they?"

"You will find your sweets and Harry's comic and Beth's hanky under the top hat on the table," said Derek. And sure enough, when Harry ran and lifted up the top hat, there were the three things

in a neat pile. The invisible Mr Pink-Whistle had slipped them there, of course.

"How do you do it? Derek, tell us how you do these marvellous tricks!" cried everyone, and even the grown-ups in the audience turned to one another, puzzled. How could a boy do such magical things?

Well, Derek did plenty more tricks, with the help of the unseen Mr Pink-Whistle, and of course Sooty the cat, who was enjoying himself immensely, and kept doing comical little dances all round the stage. He made the children laugh till they cried.

The most puzzling trick of all Derek kept till the last. "Now," he said, "I want some of you to feel in your pockets and tell me if anything is missing. Put your hands up, if you are missing something."

Everyone felt in their pockets and then hand after hand shot up. "My notebook's missing!" "My hanky's not here!" "Hey – my wallet's gone!" "I say – where's my penknife?"

"Come up on to the platform, please,

all those who have lost something," said Derek, solemnly. "I will get them back for you."

They all filed up on to the stage – three children and two puzzled grown-ups. "Stand in a line please," said Derek. "Now you, Mr Welsh – what have you lost?"

"My wallet," said Mr Welsh, anxiously.

"Hold out your hand, and I will send it back to you," said Derek, and waved his wand as Mr Welsh promptly held out his hand.

Plonk! A wallet fell into his open palm at once! Mr Welsh stood there, amazed,

unable to say a word. "Why – it came right out of the air!" said the boy next to him. "This is real magic!"

It wasn't, of course. It was just that Mr Pink-Whistle had walked quietly round the audience for a minute or two before, unseen, and taken this and that – and now, when the five people stood on the stage and asked for their things back, he simply dropped them into their waiting hands! It looked exactly as if they had fallen right out of the air. Derek kept waving his wand each time the lost things appeared, and the audience really and truly thought that he was sending their belongings back to them in some very mysterious way.

"And now," said Derek, "I've lost something. I've lost my conjuring set! Will the boy who took it from me please come up here?"

Tom, who had stolen it, sat trembling in his seat. Go up on the stage? Not he! Then he felt an invisible someone taking hold of his collar and forcing him to his feet. The someone pushed him firmly up

to the stage and stood him there, facing the audience. How he shook and shivered!

"Ah – so it was you, Tom, who took my conjuring set!" said Derek, sternly.

"I'll bring it back! I will, I promise I will!" said the terrified Tom. "Who's holding me? Someone's got hold of my shirt-collar. Let me go!"

"Very well. You can go. Bring back my conjuring set this evening – and empty your money-box and bring the money to me, to help towards the wheelchair!" bellowed Derek, suddenly, making everyone jump, Tom most of all. Pink-Whistle let go of his collar, and Tom disappeared out of the garage at top speed. Yes, yes – he would certainly give back the conjuring set, and every penny he had in his money-box, if only Derek would never play magic tricks on him again!

The audience clapped and clapped. Some of them even put more money into the box at the garage entrance as they went out. What a show!

"A black cat for an attendant – a cat that danced!" they said. "Things disappearing and flying through the air!

Whenever Derek waved his hand, something marvellous happened!"

Derek was very, very pleased with the afternoon's work. Mr Pink-Whistle made himself visible again, and they really couldn't help hugging one another.

"Grand, wasn't it?" said Pink-Whistle, chuckling. "I never enjoyed myself so much in all my life. How much money have you taken?"

"Good gracious! More than fifty pounds!" said Derek, amazed. "Mr Pink-Whistle, you must have put some in too, using your magic!"

Sooty the cat was very sorry it was all over. He and Pink-Whistle went to have tea with Derek's parents, and everyone was very happy indeed. Next week they are all going together to buy the wheelchair, because at last there is enough money.

I wish Mr Pink-Whistle would grant me a wish and let me come to the next conjuring show he helps with! I'd really love to be there!

Santa Claus Goes to Mr Pink-Whistle

One Christmas night Santa Claus went out to set off as usual in his sleigh. As soon as he stepped out of the castle door he stopped in dismay.

"What a wind!" he said, as his red coat flapped round his legs. "And my word, what snow! I'll be lucky if I find my way about tonight. Hey there, Trig and Trim – are the reindeer ready?"

Trig and Trim were the two little imps who went with Santa Claus in his sleigh. One of them drove the reindeer for him and the other helped him to tie and untie his sack of toys. They called back at once. "Yes, Santa – they're ready – but they don't like this wind and snow! They are very restless indeed!"

Santa Claus got into the sleigh and

settled down. "I'd better drive," he said, but dear me, his hands were so cold that he soon had to hand the reins to Trig.

How the wind buffeted the sleigh as it sped through the sky that night! *Whoooo-oo!* it shouted, and almost deafened Santa Claus. Then there came such a snow-squall that the reindeer couldn't see where they were going, and galloped round in circles – and the sleigh almost turned on its side.

Out fell Trig and Trim with loud yells,

and tumbled right down to earth, falling on banks of soft snow. Santa Claus had his eyes shut because of the snow and he didn't even see them go – so he was most surprised when he opened his eyes again and saw that he was the only one in the sleigh.

"Good gracious! Now what am I to do?" he thought, and he clutched at the loose reins to try to calm the reindeer. "I must get help. Things are certainly going very wrong tonight! But who can help me?"

And then he suddenly remembered dear old Mr Pink-Whistle, the little man who always puts wrong things right. "Perhaps he can do something for me," thought Santa, pulling at the reins. "Ho there, behave yourselves, reindeer – my sack of toys nearly fell out then. What would the children say if there were no toys in their stockings tomorrow morning?"

Santa Claus was a good way from where Mr Pink-Whistle lived, but the reindeer could go as fast as lightning if

they chose – and very soon the sleigh
was right over Pink-Whistle's little
cottage. Sooty, his cat, suddenly heard
the sound of the sleigh-bells and was
astonished. "Master!" he cried, running
into Pink-Whistle's room, "I can hear
Santa coming!"

"Nonsense!" said Pink-Whistle, who
was sitting cosily by the fire. "There are
no children here. You're mistaken."

But just at that moment there came a

thunderous knock at Pink-Whistle's door, and a great voice shouted loudly. "Hey, Pink-Whistle – open the door, man. It's me, Santa Claus."

Sooty and Pink-Whistle ran to the door together, astonished and delighted. Santa Claus came in, covered with snow, stamping his feet and rubbing his hands.

"Come in, come in! This is an honour!" said Pink-Whistle, gladly. "Sooty, fetch some hot drinks."

"I can't stay, Pink-Whistle," said Santa

Claus. "I've come for your help. You put things right when they go wrong, don't you?"

"I try to, sir, I always try to!" said Pink-Whistle, feeling even more surprised. "But surely you don't want my help!"

"I do, I most certainly do!" said Santa Claus. "My reindeer lost their way in this blizzard and ran round in circles, so that the sleigh almost tipped over – and Trig and Trim, my two helpers fell out."

"Good gracious!" said Pink-Whistle. "Are they hurt?"

"Oh no – they'll be all right," said Santa Claus. "There was thick snow on the ground; it'll feel like falling on a nice, soft, feather-bed, but I can't get them back, and I need help. You see, I have to keep looking at my notebook to see the names and addresses of children I am going to leave presents for, so someone must drive the reindeer – and I also need someone to tie and untie the sack for me, and hold it so that I can take out the toys I want."

"I see," said Pink-Whistle, frowning

as he thought very hard indeed. "Yes, you certainly must have help. Ah – here is Sooty with some hot drinks. What will you have, Santa – cocoa – tea – or hot lemon?"

"Well, I wouldn't mind some of all three," said Santa. "I'm so very cold. Feel my hands! How could I drive reindeer with hands as cold as that? Why, I couldn't even feel the reins!"

They sat sipping the hot drinks, and Pink-Whistle began to worry about how he could put things right for such an important person as Santa Claus. Sooty stood nearby and thought hard too.

"Well, can you think of a way to help me?" asked Santa Claus, finishing his second cup of cocoa and starting on the tea. "Don't you disappoint me now – I've heard great things of you, Pink-Whistle, yes, great things!"

"I can't think of anyone who would be able to drive reindeer through the sky," said Pink-Whistle. "I know a young air-pilot who flies planes – but reindeer are different."

94

"My dear fellow, of course they're different, but they're well-trained," said Santa. "They're as easy to drive as horses, but they go much faster. Anyone who can drive horses would do – anyone!"

"There's nobody living near here that can drive," said Pink-Whistle, beginning to feel quite desperate. "And we'd never be able to get through this blizzard to the man who keeps the riding-stables in the next village. Sooty – do you know

anyone nearby who would be able to drive Santa's reindeer?"

"Oh yes, Master!" said Sooty, at once.

"Dear me – who?" said Pink-Whistle, in surprise.

"Why, you!" said Sooty. "And even if you couldn't drive, I'm sure it would be easy to manage well-trained reindeer."

"Good gracious – yes – I suppose I could drive the sleigh!" said Pink-Whistle, suddenly excited. "Where's my thick coat, Sooty? And I shall want a woolly scarf to tie my hat on my head. And I'll keep on my warm slippers or my feet will get cold. Dear me – what an idea!"

"A very, very good one!" said Santa Claus, beaming. "It would be nice to have your company in the sleigh tonight, Pink-Whistle. You're a good fellow. I like you, and I'm not surprised that the children think of you as a friend! Right, you shall drive. But now – who can come and handle the big sack for me? What about your next-door neighbour?"

"They're away," said Pink-Whistle. But again Sooty knew what to do.

"I'm coming!" he said, and his green eyes shone brightly. "I can help with the sack. I'm used to helping Mr Pink-Whistle in all kinds of ways, Santa Claus, and I know I can help you too. Please do let me come!"

"Well, what an idea!" said Pink-Whistle, again. "Yes, I don't see why you shouldn't come, Sooty. You're very clever and always helpful. Santa Claus, I think he'll manage the sack very well for you."

"Splendid!" said the jolly old fellow, drinking the hot lemon juice. "Well, can we start now? I feel much warmer. Even my hands are beginning to warm up. Feel them!"

Pink-Whistle was soon dressed warmly in his thickest top-coat, and had his hat tied firmly on his head with a woolly scarf. He kept his comfortable slippers on, and put his woollen gloves down to the fire to warm.

"You'd better borrow one of my short coats, Sooty," said Pink-Whistle.

"Oh no – I'll be quite warm enough in my own black fur coat!" said Sooty. "I'll borrow one of your scarfs, though, Master. Are we ready now? The reindeer must be getting impatient, because I can hear their bells ringing very loudly."

Sooty put some coal on the fire, put the guard round it, turned out the lights, and off they went out of doors in to the snow.

"Thank goodness the wind isn't quite so fierce now," said Santa Claus, looking round for his reindeer. "Goodness me – is that mound over there my sleigh and reindeer? Why, they're covered with snow!"

So they were – and it was quite a job to get the snow off and climb into the sleigh. Pink-Whistle took the reins very proudly indeed, and the reindeer tossed their beautiful antlers and made their bells ring out loudly.

"You're not nervous, are you, Pink-Whistle?" asked Santa Claus.

"Not a bit," said Pink-Whistle. "This is one of the nicest jobs I've ever had to do to help anyone! Ready? Sooty, sit down, or you'll be blown out."

They set off and in half a minute were galloping through the wind-blown sky. The snow had almost stopped falling now, so it was much easier to see the way. The reindeer knew it well, for they had galloped the same way for hundreds of years.

Pink-Whistle enjoyed himself very much indeed. So did Sooty – in fact, Sooty felt very important whenever he had to open the sack for Santa, and then tie it up safely again. Santa always knew exactly what to take out of it.

"See – I have a long list," he said to Sooty, and showed it to him. "I've written down on it all the things the children have asked me for. This boy John now, that we've just taken an aeroplane for out of the sack – here's his name – and see, I've written 'Aeroplane' down beside it. I'd never remember all these things without my list. Thank goodness it didn't blow away in the wind! Now – I'll just climb down this chimney if you'll hold the reindeer still on the roof, Pink-Whistle. I've trained them not to stamp about on roofs, so they'll be quite quiet."

It was really a very exciting night for Mr Pink-Whistle and Sooty. They had never enjoyed themselves so much in all

their lives. Sooty thought the sack of toys was marvellous – it always seemed as full as ever, no matter how many toys Santa took out of it.

"One child has asked for a clockwork mouse," said Santa to Sooty. "Aha! That's the kind of toy you'd like, wouldn't you! Now, just let me look at my list again. We're getting on!"

When all the toys had been put into the stockings of many, many children, Pink-Whistle drove back to his own little house again, and got out of the sleigh very regretfully. Sooty jumped out too, and ran indoors to fetch lumps of sugar for the reindeer.

"Can you drive yourself back home now, Santa?" asked Pink-Whistle. "Let me feel your hands. Yes, they are lovely and warm."

"Oh, I'll be all right now," said Santa. "The wind had dropped and it's much warmer – and I shan't have to delve into my sack any more. I shall just sit back in my seat and hold the reins loosely and let the reindeer gallop back home at top speed."

"I have enjoyed going out with you on Christmas Eve and driving your reindeer," said Pink-Whistle.

"Well, I'll know where to come to next time things go wrong," said Santa Claus, shaking the reins and clicking to the reindeer, who were now all munching Sooty's lumps of sugar. "Many, many thanks. Goodbye, Pink-Whistle, goodbye, Sooty!"

And with a ringing of bells they were off! Pink-Whistle and Sooty couldn't help feeling sad that their grand adventure was over. They went indoors together – and will you believe it, there, on the table, was a present for each of them!

"A new top hat for me – and a great big clockwork mouse for you, Sooty!" said Pink-Whistle in surprise. "How did Santa put them here without us knowing? Well – isn't he a grand old fellow!"

Yes, Mr Pink-Whistle, he is – and so are you!

Mr Pink-Whistle and the Money-Box

For some time Mr Pink-Whistle hadn't come across anything to put right, and he was feeling very pleased about it.

"Perhaps the world is getting a better place," he thought to himself. "Perhaps people are being nicer to one another, and kinder. Maybe I needn't go around any more looking for things to put right. Perhaps I can go back to my own little cottage and live there peacefully with Sooty, my cat."

But that very day Pink-Whistle had to change his mind, because he found two very unhappy children.

Pink-Whistle was walking in the lane that ran to the back of their garden, and he heard one of the children crying.

"Never mind," said a boy's voice.

"Never mind, Katie. We shall have to save up again, that's all."

"But it was such a mean thing to do to us," sobbed Katie. "That's what's making me cry. It was such a horrid, mean, unkind thing."

Pink-Whistle peeped over the wall. He saw two children nearby – a boy and a girl. They both looked very upset, but the boy wasn't crying.

"What's the matter?" asked Pink-Whistle. "Can I do anything to help?"

"No, I'm afraid not," said the boy. "You

see, it's like this. Katie and I have been saving up for our mother's birthday. We know exactly what she wants – that big red shawl in the dress shop. It's a lovely one."

"I know. I've seen it," said Pink-Whistle.

"Well, it costs a lot of money," said the boy. "But Katie and I have been doing all kinds of jobs to earn the money for it."

"We ran errands and we delivered papers," said Katie, rubbing her eyes.

"I helped the farmer to lift his potatoes," said the boy. "And that's hard work."

"And I took Mrs Brown's baby out each day for a week when she was ill," said Katie. "She gave me five pounds for that."

"And I weeded old Mr Kent's garden, and he gave me three pounds," said the boy. "We put it all into our money-box pig."

"Oh, was your money-box in the shape of a pig?" asked Mr Pink-Whistle. "I like that sort of money-box."

"It was a tin pig, painted pink, and it had a slot in its back," said Katie. "And it had a sort of little key hanging on its tail to unlock a sort of little door in its tummy. We got the money out of the little door when we wanted it."

"The pig was so nice and full," said the boy. "It jingled when we shook it. We were sure we had nearly enough to buy the shawl, and it's Mum's birthday next week. But now all our money is gone!"

"Where's it gone?" said Pink-Whistle, surprised.

"Someone stole it," said Katie, her eyes filling with tears again. "We took it out here in the garden, meaning to count out the money. Then Mummy called us in for our biscuits and we ran indoors, and when we came out the pig was gone, and all the money with it."

"Somebody must have come by, looked over the wall, and seen the money-box pig," said the boy, sadly. "Now all our hard work is wasted and we shall never get enough money to buy that shawl."

"It really is a shame," said Mr Pink-Whistle, getting quite red with anger. "It's not fair that someone should come along and take all the money you've worked so hard to get. Perhaps I have got some for you. Wait a minute. Let me look in my pockets."

But Pink-Whistle had only sixty pence that day, so that wasn't much use. He rubbed one of his pointed ears and frowned. What could he do? He must do something.

Someone called the children. "We must go," said Katie. "It's time for our lunch.

Thank you for being so nice."

The children ran off. Mr Pink-Whistle went on down the lane, remembering the girl's tear-stained face and the boy's look of disappointment. What a shame to steal from children!

"Well, I shall do something!" said Pink-Whistle, fiercely. "But I don't know what. It seems to me as if all I can do is poke my nose into every house I see, and try to find that money-box pig!"

So he made himself invisible, and began to peep into the windows of all the houses he passed. But he didn't see any money-box pig at all.

He went on and on, peeping into kitchens and sitting-rooms, trying to discover a money-box pig – and at last he found one!

It was standing on the mantelpiece of a neat little cottage, next to a ticking clock. There was a man in the room, reading. He looked smart and clean and neat – but Pink-Whistle didn't really like his face.

"Too clever!" thought Pink-Whistle.

"Too sharp! He looks as if he would do people a bad turn if he could, and think himself clever to do it! And there's the money-box pig, standing on the mantelpiece. Can it be that pig the children had stolen from them? Surely this well-dressed man here wouldn't steal such a thing as a child's money-box? He looks quite well off."

Someone went up the path and knocked at the door. The man inside looked up, got up quickly, took the money-box pig and put it under a cushion. Then Pink-Whistle knew he

had stolen it. "Aha!" said the little man to himself, "Aha! He wouldn't hide it if he hadn't stolen it. The mean fellow!"

The man opened the door to his friend, and Pink-Whistle slipped in beside him. He was quite invisible, so no one knew he was there.

"You're early," said the first man. "The others haven't arrived yet."

"Oho!" thought Pink-Whistle. "So there is to be a meeting. I think I'll stay – and have a bit of fun!"

So he stood in a corner and then, when he had a chance to do it, he slipped his hand under the cushion and took out the pig. He stood it on the mantelpiece.

He shook it and the money jingled. Then Pink-Whistle made a grunting noise, just like a little pig, and spoke in a funny piggy voice.

"Take me back, take me back!"

Mr Crooky, the man who lived in the cottage, looked up, very startled, and so did his friend. It seemed to them as if the money-box pig on the mantelpiece was jigging up and down and talking.

They couldn't see Pink-Whistle moving it, of course.

"How extraordinary!" said the friend. Mr Crooky got up and took hold of the pig very roughly. He took it into the kitchen and put it on the dresser there. He slammed the door and came back. There was a knock at the front door and two more men came into the meeting.

Pink-Whistle grinned. He slipped quietly into the kitchen, found the pig, came back, shut the kitchen door softly, and, when no one was looking, placed the pig on the mantelpiece again!

Then he jiggled it hard and grunted in a piggy way again, talking in a funny, squeaky voice. "Take me back! Take me back! I don't belong to you. Take me back!"

All the four men stopped talking and stared in astonishment at the jiggling pig. Mr Crooky went very red and looked most alarmed. How had that pig got down from the dresser, opened the kitchen door, and got back to the mantelpiece? How was it that it grunted and jiggled and talked like that? It must be magic!

"What does it mean, saying that it wants to be taken back?" asked one of the men. "Doesn't it belong to you?"

"Of course it does," said Mr Crooky. "I can't imagine what's come over the pig. I never knew a tin pig behave like that before."

"Oh, you bad story-teller, oh, you wicked man!" squeaked Pink-Whistle, making the pig dance all round the mantelpiece, as if it was angry. "You stole me! You know you did! Take me back, take me back!"

"This is very strange," said one of the men, looking hard at Crooky. "What does it mean?"

"Nothing. It's just a silly joke of some sort," said Mr Crooky, beginning to tremble. "I'll throw the pig in the dustbin."

So he snatched it up, went into the yard and threw the pig hard into the dustbin. He slammed on the lid and went

back into the house. How tiresome of this to happen just when he had called a meeting to ask his friends to give him money to start a shop! Now they might not trust him!

Pink-Whistle has gone into the yard with Mr Crooky. As soon as Crooky had gone back, Pink-Whistle took off the lid and fished out the pig. It was covered with tea leaves.

Pink-Whistle crept to the window. It was open. To the men's enormous surprise, the money-box pig suddenly appeared on the windowsill, jiggling and jumping like mad, and a grunting voice could be heard at the same time. Then came the squeaky, piggy voice.

"You bad man! You put me in the dustbin! I'm covered with tea leaves – but you ought to be covered with shame! You stole from those children. You know you did. Take me back, take me back!"

"This is most extraordinary and most disgraceful," said one of the men, standing up. "Mr Crooky, take that pig back at once. If you don't, I shall call the village policeman and ask him to listen to all the pig says."

Mr Crooky felt as if he were in a bad dream. He stared at the pig, which turned a somersault and rattled like mad. "I'm hungry!" it squeaked, "I'm hungry. You put something in me, quick! I'm hungreeeeeeeeeeey!"

Mr Crooky felt so frightened that he put his hand into his pocket and pulled out the money there. He popped it into the slot in the pig's back.

"More, more!" cried the pig, and Mr

Crooky put in more and more until he had no money left. "Now take me home, home, home!" cried the pig, and leaped high into the air and back again to the windowsill. Mr Crooky thought that either he or the pig must be mad, or perhaps both of them. Or maybe it was a frightening kind of dream.

"Well, I'd better take you back, and then perhaps I shall wake up," he said. So he snatched up the dancing pig and ran off with it at top speed. He came to the children's garden and threw the pig over the wall. It landed on the grass.

Mr Crooky turned to go home. "Now don't you ever do such a wicked thing again!" boomed a voice in his ear, making him almost jump out of his skin. It was Mr Pink-Whistle, of course, having one last go at Mr Crooky. The man tore off down the lane as if a hundred dogs were after him. Mr Pink-Whistle made himself visible and climbed over the wall into the garden. He called the children.

They came running to him and he showed them the pig, which he had

picked up. "Here you are," he said. "Safely back again – and heavier than before."

The children shouted with delight. They undid the little door in the pig's tummy and the money tumbled out. What a lot there was now!

"More than we ever put in!" cried Katie. "Oh, how marvellous! How did it happen, little man? Tell us, do!"

But Pink-Whistle had vanished again. He didn't need to be thanked. It was enough to see the children's joyful faces, and to know that they could buy their mother the present they had saved up for – and could buy her something else besides now!

As for Mr Crooky, he didn't get the money lent to him for the shop he wanted to start – and a very good thing, too! He is still puzzled whenever he thinks of that grunting, dancing, talking pig, but if he happens to read this story, he won't be puzzled any more!

Mr Pink-Whistle
Goes to School

Mr Pink-Whistle was walking down the road wondering if the fishmonger had any kippers for himself and Sooty, his cat, when four girls and two boys came running along.

"Quick," said one. "Get round the corner before Harry and George see us!"

They shot round the corner – and then came the sound of pattering footsteps behind Mr Pink-Whistle once more, and along came two big boys, almost knocking him over.

Mr Pink-Whistle went spinning into the gutter and just saved himself from sitting down hard by clutching at a lamppost.

The two boys didn't say they were sorry, they didn't even stop! They rushed round the corner after the smaller children.

"Good gracious!" said Mr Pink-Whistle, letting go of the lamppost. "What unpleasant boys! Who are they, I wonder?"

He went round the corner. He saw Harry and George pouncing on the smaller children and taking their hats and caps away. They sent them sailing up into the trees and over the hedges!

"You *are* hateful," said a small girl, beginning to cry. "You're always playing horrid tricks and making us take the blame!"

"You hid my French book yesterday and I got into trouble for it," said Jean.

"You spilled my drink all over the floor, and I had to stay in," said Peter. "I know you did it! It's just the kind of thing you always do."

"Yes – and then you leave us to take the blame," said Diana. "And if we tell tales of you you pinch our faces and stamp on our toes!"

Harry pounced on Diana and pulled

her hair so hard that she squealed.

"Let go!" she said.

Mr Pink-Whistle made himself invisible. He crept up to Harry, caught hold of his hair and tugged hard.

"Oh!" said Harry, and swung round. George was just near by. "Did you pull my hair? What do you think you're doing?"

"I didn't touch you," said George. "Don't be silly!"

Then the two boys glared at one another and put up their fists to fight.

The other children saw their chance and ran off at once. Let them fight! They wouldn't bother the others then!

Mr Pink-Whistle didn't like the two boys at all. He took a look at them. Their faces were hard. It wouldn't be any good talking to them, or pleading with them to be better. They would laugh.

"No – the only thing is to do the same things to them that they do to others," decided Mr Pink-Whistle. "I shall go to school with these children this afternoon. Ha – there'll be a bit of fun then! But not for George and Harry!"

He waited for the children that afternoon and then walked along beside them, unseen. He saw how they all ran away from George and Harry, and how frightened of the two big boys they were.

"A couple of bullies!" said Mr Pink-Whistle. "Well, well – bullies are always cowards, so we'll just see what Harry and George do when unpleasant things begin to happen to them. They shall take the blame for things I do this afternoon, in return for making others take the blame for things that they so often have done."

He went into the schoolroom with Harry and George and the rest of their class. He noticed where the two big boys sat and went over to them. Nobody could see him. He was invisible of course.

When George was bending down to pick up a dropped pencil Mr Pink-Whistle opened his desk lid and let it drop with a terrific bang!

Everyone jumped. The teacher frowned. "George! There's no need to

make that noise," she said.

"I didn't," said George, indignantly. "I was bending down. Someone else must have banged my desk-lid."

"Was it you, Harry?" asked the teacher. Harry always sat next to George.

"No, it wasn't," said Harry, rudely.

Well, Mr Pink-Whistle managed to bang George's desk-lid twice more and the teacher began to blame Harry, because George was so very indignant that she felt sure it couldn't be his fault.

The two boys glared at one another. Then Mr Pink-Whistle tipped a pile of books off Harry's desk when he wasn't looking!

"Harry!" said the teacher.

"I didn't do it," said Harry, angrily. "Make George pick up my books. He must have done that."

"I didn't," said George. "Yah!"

"Boys, boys!" said the teacher. "George, come up here and write on the board for me. Write down the homework notes for tomorrow."

George went up sulkily. He took up

the chalk and began to write on the
board. Mr Pink-Whistle was just behind
him, invisible.

He took George's hand and began to
guide the piece of chalk. And do you
know what he wrote? He wrote this:

*Harry is a silly donkey. Harry is a
dunce. Harry is...*

George was horrified. Whatever was
the chalk doing? It seemed to be writing
by itself and he couldn't stop it. And look

what it was writing too. Whatever would his teacher say? Where was the duster? He must rub out the rude writing at once!

Aha! Mr Pink-Whistle had taken the duster, of course. He had thrown it up to the top of a picture. George couldn't see it anywhere.

The children saw what George had written, and they began to nudge one another and giggle. The teacher turned to see what George was doing behind her – and, she saw what he had written on the board!

"George!" she said angrily. "How dare you do that? What in the world are you thinking of? Rub it out at once."

"I didn't mean to," said poor George. "It felt as if the chalk was writing by itself."

"Oh, don't be silly," said the teacher. "My goodness me – look where the duster has been thrown to! Did you throw it there, George? You'd better lose ten marks straight away for your silly behaviour this afternoon!"

Harry laughed like anything. He was angry with George for writing rude things about him on the board. Mr Pink-Whistle waited till George was back in his seat and then he pulled Harry's hair quite hard.

Harry jumped up and glared round at George. Mr Pink-Whistle tugged at George's hair then. George jumped up and glared round at Harry.

"Stop that!" they said to each other, and the teacher banged on her desk for quiet.

Well, Mr Pink-Whistle quite enjoyed

himself that afternoon and so did all the class, except Harry and George. Harry's ruler shot off the desk. George's pencil-box upset all over the floor. Harry's shoe-laces came mysteriously undone three times. George's socks kept slipping down to his ankles, and his shirt buttons came undone at the neck. It was all very extraordinary.

They all went out to play for ten minutes. Mr Pink-Whistle went with them. He kicked Harry's ball into the next-door garden. He tripped George up twice and sent him rolling over and over. The two boys got very angry indeed, because they both felt certain it was the other playing tricks.

After a few minutes, Mr Pink-Whistle went indoors. He went to Harry's desk and put half his books into George's. He put George's pencils into Harry's box. That was the kind of thing the two boys were always doing to other people. Well, let them see if they liked it or not!

They didn't like it a bit. Harry wailed aloud when he found half his books gone,

because the teacher was always very cross when anyone was careless with books. And George was furious to find his best pencils missing.

"Who's taken them? Wait till I find out!" he cried angrily. "Teacher – all my best pencils have gone!"

They were found in Harry's box almost at once, and George almost flew at him in a rage. He would have hit him there and then if the teacher hadn't suddenly discovered that Harry's books were in George's desk! She was really disgusted with the goings-on.

"I thought you two boys were friends. Look at this – your books in George's desk, Harry, and all George's pencils in your box. You ought to be ashamed of yourselves. Any more nonsense from either of you and you will stay in for half an hour."

Well, there was quite a lot of nonsense of course – but it was from Mr-Pink-Whistle, not from the boys. He upset George's paint-pot all over his painting – a thing that George himself did to somebody almost every painting lesson! And he smudged Harry's best writing

when he wasn't looking. And that, too, was something that Harry was very fond of doing to the smaller children.

Their teacher was cross. "Stay in for half an hour, both of you," she said. "I don't care if you are going out to a party. You can be half an hour late."

"But you know it's my cousin's birthday party," said George, indignantly. "I can't be late."

"I know all about the party – and I'm afraid you will be late, both of you!" said the teacher, firmly. The two boys glared at one another. Each felt sure it was the other who had got him into all this trouble!

They had to stay in for half an hour and do most of their work again. Then they said a sulky goodbye and went out.

As soon as they got out in the road they began to quarrel. "I suppose you think you were very clever this afternoon!" said George, angrily. "Well, take that!"

And he hit Harry hard on the back. Mr Pink-Whistle grinned. A fight? Well, he would join in as well. He would repay both George and Harry for the nasty treatment they had many a time dealt out to the younger children.

So, quite invisible, he hopped in and out, dealing a punch here and a tug there, and making the boys yell in pain, and go for each other all the more.

Biff! That was George hitting Harry on the nose. It began to bleed.

Smack! That was Harry hitting George on his right eye. It began to go black at once.

Thud! That was Mr Pink-Whistle doing his share!

Biff-Bang! That was both boys at once – and they fell over, *crash*, into a muddy puddle. They sat up, howling.

"Let's stop," wept George. "My eye hurts. And your nose is bleeding. We're terribly late for the party. We shall miss all the good things at tea."

So, sniffing and snuffling, muddy, wet and very much the worse for wear, the two boys arrived at George's cousin's house. But when his aunt saw them, she

was very cross indeed. "George, Harry! How can you come to a party looking like that? Have you been fighting one another? You should be ashamed of yourselves. One with a black eye and one with a bleeding nose! I won't let you in. You shan't come to the party!"

And she slammed the door in their faces. They went howling down the street, very sorry for themselves.

Mr Pink-Whistle began to think they might have learned their lesson. He suddenly appeared beside them, a kind little man with pointed ears.

"Come and have tea with me," he said. "I live not far off with my cat, Sooty."

So they went with him, still sniffing. He made them wash and brush their hair. He stopped Harry's nose from bleeding and he bathed George's eye. Then he sat them down to bread and butter and honey and a sponge cake.

"You're very kind," said George, surprised.

"I'm not always," said Mr Pink-Whistle, solemnly. "Sometimes, when I see mean, unkind people I get that way myself – just to punish them, you know. I've had a good time this afternoon, punishing two nasty little boys. My word, they were horrid things – always teasing the smaller ones and getting them into trouble."

The two boys gazed at him, afraid.

"You've no idea of the things I did," said Mr Pink-Whistle, passing them the cake. "My, the tricks I played in their class this afternoon – and what a time I had when those boys fought. I fought too – biff, thud!"

The boys looked at one another uncomfortably. They both felt very scared.

"You know, I always think that if mean, unkind people get treated meanly and unkindly themselves sometimes, they learn how horrid it is," said Mr Pink-Whistle. "Of course, they sometimes need more than one lesson – perhaps two, or four, or even six!"

He looked hard at the two boys. They looked back. "Sir," said George, in a small voice, "we shan't need more than one lesson. I promise you that."

"I promise you, too," said Harry, in a whisper. "It's – it's very kind of you to take us home and give us this tea – when you know we're mean."

"Bless us all, you can come again as often as you like – so long as you don't need another lesson from me, but only a nice tea!" said kind Mr Pink-Whistle. "Now do take another piece of cake each, just to show there's no ill-feeling between us!"

Well, they did of course. And, so far as

I know, Mr Pink-Whistle hasn't had to give them another lesson – yet! But he would, you know, if they broke their promise. He's kind but he's fierce, too, when he's putting wrong things right!

Sooty Helps
Mr Pink-Whistle

Every morning Mr Pink-Whistle took a
little walk after breakfast. He went out of
his front gate, turned to the right down
the lane, and then, when he came to the
stile, he climbed over it to go across the
fields.

One morning he set off as usual. It
was a cold day and Sooty, his cat, had
brought him his hat and a warm scarf.
Mr Pink-Whistle set off quickly down
the lane, looking out for late blackberries
as he went.

He came to the stile and climbed over.
He was surprised to see a big brown
horse in the field, standing quite still,
looking rather miserable. The farmer
had just left him there, and Pink-Whistle
called to him.

"Hey – is that a new horse of yours?"

"Oh no," said the farmer. "He's old but he's been a good worker. Barney is his name. He's hurt one of his legs so he's no use now for work."

"Will he just live in this field then?" said Pink-Whistle. "Will he always be here? I'll bring him an apple or two, if so. I always come this way in the mornings."

"That's kind of you," said the farmer. "He's used to company, you see – he'll be lonely without the other horses and the farm-men all round him." He patted the horse and then went out of the field.

Pink-Whistle patted him too, and then stroked the long velvety nose.

"You'll enjoy your rest, Barney," he said. "I'll come and see you each day, so don't be lonely."

Every day Pink-Whistle spoke to old Barney when he went across the field. He always had a little present for him – sometimes an apple, sometimes a crust of bread or a lump of sugar. Barney looked for him each day, and was sad when the little man had gone. He was very lonely.

He missed all the other horses he knew and longed to be back at the farm, working with his friends. Sometimes he heard one of them clip-clopping down the near-by lane, and would run to the gate and neigh loudly – "Wait for me! I want to come with you! Wait!"

But the other horse couldn't stop, and Barney would stand at the gate, his head down, wondering why he couldn't work for the farmer any more, or talk to the other horses and rub noses with them.

Pink-Whistle was sad to see Barney looking so lonely. "Cheer up!" he said,

stroking the long nose. "You've worked so hard all your life long that you ought to be glad of a rest now. It's a pity none of your friends can be with you – but I suppose they're in their stables at night."

Barney hardly lifted his head to look at Pink-Whistle. He didn't even nibble at the apple the little man had brought. Pink-Whistle felt very worried.

"You're moping," he said. "You're getting thin and weak. You stand all day with your head down, hardly moving. Cheer up, Barney, do cheer up!"

Pink-Whistle went to the farmer. "That nice old horse of yours is moping terribly," he said. "He's so very lonely. There's no one to love him and no one for him to love. No other animal to play with or talk to – all alone, all day and all night. He'll die of sadness!"

"Well, his field is too far away to take my other horses to after their work is done," said the farmer, "and I'm to busy to go and cosset him! He's lucky to have a field of his own and no work to do. Many a farmer would have sold him to be killed."

"Yes – yes, I suppose so," said Pink-Whistle, sadly. "But it worries me to see him standing alone all day long, looking miserable."

"I've far bigger worries that that!" said the farmer. "I'm not an unkind man, Pink-Whistle; but I simply haven't time to worry about one old horse who's lonely, when I have at least a hundred problems each day to see to. If you feel so worried about him, well, do something yourself! You like to put things right, don't you?"

"Yes. Yes, I do," said Pink-Whistle. "But

I can't for the life of me see how to put this thing right, and yet I can't bear to watch that nice old horse getting thinner and more miserable every day!"

"Well, I've my cows to milk now," said the farmer. "I can't stop a minute longer!" And away he went at top speed to his cowshed, where his twenty cows were waiting to be milked.

Sooty the cat saw his master looking so sad that evening that he wondered what the matter was.

"Master – it isn't like you to be so mopey!" he said. "You're as sad as that old horse in the field!"

"Well, I can't help thinking about him," said Pink-Whistle. "He's so lonely. He'll soon lie down and die of loneliness and boredom! And I can't think how to put things right for him. Here am I, always going about the world putting wrong things right and I can't even make that old horse happy."

"I'll try to help you, Master," said Sooty, and patted Pink-Whistle with a soft little paw. "Cheer up – I'll make you a nice cup of coffee before I go out. I'd like to see what it feels like to put a wrong thing right; so I'll look around and see if there's something I can do for old Barney."

"Well, if I can't, I don't expect you can, Sooty, though you're a very clever cat," said Pink-Whistle, with a sigh. "I could hardly get to sleep last night for thinking about the poor old fellow."

Sooty made Mr Pink-Whistle a cup of coffee and then trotted off to see his friend in the next village. His name was Whiskers, and he belonged to the greengrocer there. He was very pleased

to see Sooty, and soon the two cats were on their favourite wall, basking in the autumn sunshine.

"Any news, Whiskers?" asked Sooty. "Have you been out in the cart lately?"

Whiskers sometimes used to go out sitting beside his master in the greengrocer's cart. Sooty had hoped and hoped that he would be asked to do this one day, but Whiskers hadn't even suggested such a thing. No – he was going to be the only cat who rode in a cart.

"I haven't much news," said Whiskers. "And it's not much fun going out in the cart now, either. Poor old Neddy-donkey

147

is so very slow nowadays!"

Neddy was the little donkey who drew the greengrocer's cart – a sturdy little grey animal with long furry ears and a tail that whisked about.

"Why? What's the matter with Neddy?" asked Sooty, in surprise. "He's usually so spry."

"Well, he's old now," said Whiskers, "and too slow for the cart."

"What will happen to dear old Neddy?" asked Sooty. "Will he give children rides on the beach?"

"No," said Whiskers, looking suddenly sad. "No. Something dreadful is going to happen to him."

"What?" asked Sooty.

"Well, you see, we've no field to keep him in – and so – so – oh dear, I hardly like to tell you, Sooty. No, I can't tell you."

"Whiskers – you don't mean that dear old Neddy will be sent away to be killed, do you?" cried Sooty, almost falling off the wall in horror. 'Oh no – not dear old Neddy! He's such a darling."

"I know. But my master says he can't afford to pay stabling fees for a donkey that's too slow to work," said Whiskers.

"There's an old horse near where we live who can't work now, too," said Sooty sadly. "And the farmer has put him into a field all by himself, and he's so miserable. Oh dear, I don't like it when these things happen. Animals can't help getting old, can they? Thank goodness the farmer didn't send dear old Barney away to be killed – though really he's so miserable he might be happier dead!"

"I though your master, Mr Pink-Whistle, could always put wrong things right," said Whiskers. "Couldn't he do something for that old horse, and perhaps for our Neddy-donkey too?"

"No. He said he couldn't think of anything at all," said Sooty. "It's the very first time he hasn't been able to put a wrong thing right. Let's change the subject and talk of something else, Whiskers. I feel sad."

So they chatted about the dog next door, and of the best way to catch rats, and what a nuisance it was that rabbits could go down holes so easily – and then Sooty said it was time he went.

"I hope dear old Neddy will still be here when you next come to see me," said Whiskers, solemnly. "But if I don't mention him, you'll know what's happened, and mustn't ask me, because it would make me too sad."

Sooty went home to Mr Pink-Whistle feeling rather sad himself. He went by the field where old Barney stood, and looked through the gate at him. There was the old horse, thinner than ever, his head hanging down, standing quite still.

Sooty ran on, thinking of poor old Neddy and lonely Barney, and then, just as he went in at the gate, a wonderful idea came to him. He gave a yowl of delight and ran straight into the room where Pink-Whistle was sitting.

"Master! Oh, Master, I believe I know how to put a wrong thing right! I believe I—"

"Now, now – don't get so excited," said Pink-Whistle, surprised. "What's all this about?"

"Master! My friend Whiskers told me that that dear little Neddy-donkey is going to be sent away to be killed!" cried Sooty. "And listen, you know how lonely poor old Barney is now! Well – why can't that little donkey come and live with Barney in his field? There's plenty of grass for both of them. Then Neddy could be happy and have a rest and Barney wouldn't be lonely and sad any more, because he would have someone to talk to and play with!"

Pink-Whistle stared at the excited little cat. A broad smile came over his round face. "Sooty, I believe you've solved our problem!" he said. "Yes – I really believe you have! I'll go and see the greengrocer straight away, and then I'll see the farmer."

So off went Pink-Whistle at once. He saw the greengrocer, and the man nodded his head.

"Fine, fine!" he said. "I'd like my old Neddy-donkey to have company and a quiet old age. He can come tomorrow, if you like – if the farmer agrees."

Well, the farmer agreed at once, of course. "Just the thing for old Barney!" he said. "He'll love a companion – especially that dear little donkey. Let him come tomorrow."

So Pink-Whistle trotted off the next day to fetch Neddy-donkey, and the two of them trotted back and soon came to Barney's field. Pink-Whistle opened the gate and let little Neddy through. The donkey stood looking in delight at the sunny, grassy field. What a beautiful place! Much, much better than his dark stable! But who was that over there,

standing tall and still, with his head hanging down?

"A horse! A big horse," thought Neddy. "I suppose this field belongs to him. Will he mind my being here? I'd better ask him."

So away he trotted to Barney, and brayed politely. Barney lifted his head, most surprised to see the donkey, so much smaller than he was.

"Please, big horse – is this your field?" asked Neddy. "Mr Pink-Whistle said I could come and live here. But I won't if you want to be by yourself. I'm only a

little rather stupid donkey, not a fine horse like you."

Barney looked at the pretty little donkey, whose big brown eyes stared at him so trustfully. He suddenly whinnied and threw up his head.

"Stay with me! I'll look after you, you're so small. I'll show you the best tree to stand under when it rains. I'll show you where there's a little stream over yonder to drink from. Do, do stay here with me and be my friend. I'm so lonely."

Barney put down his head and rubbed the little donkey's grey furry nose with his. Neddy was suddenly so happy that he brayed loudly, and then threw up his heels and galloped all round Barney.

"Ee-aw! Ee-aw! Catch me!" he cried, and away he went round the field. Barney whinnied again and then suddenly ran after him, and soon the two were racing round the field together. Then they stood still, and Barney put his big head down over the little donkey's neck, and they stood there together, perfectly happy. Pink-Whistle felt tears coming into his eyes because he was so happy, too.

"Well, fancy two wrong things being put right so quickly!" he said to himself. "Good little Sooty – this was his idea. Oh, I do hope they'll be real friends!"

Well, they are! Barney loves the little donkey with all his heart, and Neddy thinks the world of his big friend too. They eat together and drink together, and lie down together to sleep, as happy as can be. Old Barney is fat again and as lively as ever he used to be.

"It's nice to put wrong things right, isn't it, Master?" said Sooty. "It's such a lovely warm feeling!"

You're right, little Sooty – it is!

Mr Pink-Whistle
Gets a Laugh

Mr Pink-Whistle had been to see an old friend of his, and had just said goodbye.

"I must catch the bus!" he said. "I shall be late for lunch if I don't, and Sooty, my cat, won't be very pleased!"

But just as he reached the corner where the bus stop was, he saw the bus rumbling away down the road. He had missed it!

"Never mind – I'll buy some sandwiches and go and eat them in this park," he thought, and off he went to get some sardine and tomato sandwiches. Then he made his way to the park, and sat down on a seat.

It was sunny and warm, and Mr Pink-Whistle felt happy. He sat there eating his sandwiches, throwing crumbs to the sparrows and chaffinches around. And then he felt sleepy.

He closed his eyes and nodded a little. Soon he was dreaming, and in his dream he heard someone crying.

"Don't! Don't!" he heard, and woke up with a jump. A little girl was coming down the path, with tears running down her cheeks. Mr Pink-Whistle sat up straight at once. Was there something here that he could put right?

"Hello, hello!" said Pink-Whistle, as the little girl came by. "What's wrong?"

"He's taken my biscuits," said the little girl. "And he's eaten them!"

"Dear me – who has?" said Mr Pink-Whistle, wishing that he hadn't eaten all his sandwiches, so that he could offer the little girl some.

"That boy – the boy who rushes out at us," said the little girl, crying again. "I don't know his name. He hides in the bushes while we're playing and then he rushes out and takes our things. There's another boy, too, this morning. They took Peter's ball and Louise's balloon."

"Look, here's some money to buy some more biscuits," said Pink-Whistle. "Don't cry any more. I'll see to those boys."

"Oh, thank you!" said the small girl and she scrubbed her wet cheeks with her hanky. "They're up there, look – by the children's playground. But you'd better be careful. They might knock off your hat and run away with it!"

"Good gracious me!" said Pink-Whistle, astonished. He thought he would go over to the children's playground and watch for these two boys.

"I'll make myself invisible," thought Mr Pink-Whistle. "Then there won't be any chance of my hat being knocked off. So that's the kind of boys they are, is it? Aha – they certainly need someone to deal with them!"

He muttered a few magic words under his breath, and hey presto, he was gone! Not a bit of him was to be seen; he was quite invisible. He set off up the path towards the children's playground, listening to the calls and shouts that came from there. It sounded as if quite a lot of children were playing games.

He came to a seat just by the playground and sat down. there were swings and see-saws there, There were children playing with bats and balls, there was even a pond where some were sailing little boats. Pink-Whistle watched. He couldn't see any bad boys at all. Everyone seemed to be playing happily. Then he saw a boy coming up the path to go to the pond, carrying a little ship with a sail. Mr Pink-Whistle was watching him when there came a rustle in the bushes behind him, and out leaped a big boy, making Pink-Whistle jump almost out of his skin.

He pushed the small boy over, snatched his ship, and leaped back into the bushes. There was a sound of giggling and whispering, and Pink-Whistle guessed the second boy was there too.

The other boy sat up, dazed, for he had knocked his head on the path. "Where's my ship?" he shouted. "Give it back to me!"

But nobody came to give it back, and he went mournfully to the playground, looking everywhere for someone with his ship. Then out came the two boys from the bushes, nudging one another and giggling. One of them had the ship. They walked boldly over to the pond and set the boat on the water.

The boy who owned the ship came up at once. "That's mine!" he said. "You snatched it from me just now. You give it back."

"Ooh, you fibber! It's ours," said the two boys together. "You just try and get it from us. We'll knock you over!"

Other children came round. "I bet you took his ship!" cried a small girl with a pram. "You took my brother's cap the other day. I saw you!"

One of the big boys reached over to the pram, took out the doll that sat there and threw it into the water – *splash*! The

girl screamed. But nobody dared to do anything to the two big boys. Another boy waded into the water and brought back the doll for the little girl, but just as he handed it to her, the second big boy snatched it and once again the poor doll was thrown into the water.

And then, to Pink-Whistle's delight, up came the park-keeper! "Now, now!" he said. "What's all this? Are you making nuisances of yourselves again, you boys? Clear off at once!"

The park-keeper was a little man, and the two boys laughed at him. One gave him a push that almost sent him into the pond, and the other knocked off his peaked cap. All the children watched in silence.

"Now then! You stop that! I'll report you!" shouted the little park-keeper angrily. "Get my cap!"

"Get it yourself!" said one of the boys. "Report us! Why, you don't even know our names!"

The park-keeper ran at him, but the boy dodged and took to his heels, followed

by his friend. They could run fast and they disappeared round the bushes at top speed.

"They haven't gone home," said another boy. "I'll bet they're waiting till the park-keeper's gone, then they'll be here again. I wish a policeman would come."

The park-keeper went off, fuming with rage, and the children began to play again. Mr Pink-Whistle kept a careful watch – were those bad boys anywhere near? He hoped so. He was going to have a bit of fun with them!

Yes, there they were in those bushes. Ah – here they came, giggling and pushing one another. They ran at a boy with a cricket bat and pulled it out of his hand. They took a ball from someone else and began to have a game. If anyone came near they swiped at him with the bat.

Mr Pink-Whistle got up. He was still invisible, and he walked among the children unseen. He went up to the big boy with the bat and twisted it out of his hand. The boy stared in amazement. "Here, who took my bat? Hey – what's happening?"

Pink-Whistle was holding the bat but as he was invisible, it looked just as if the bat were hanging by itself in the air! Pink-Whistle raised it as if to give the boy a smart rap with it. The boy yelled.

Then Pink-Whistle snatched off the boy's cap and ran away with it. It looked strange to see a cap bobbing along by itself in the air! Pink-Whistle put it on the head of the little statue on the water fountain. How strange it was to see a cap put itself there! Nobody could see Pink-Whistle, of course.

The little man went back to the two surprised boys. He undid the tie belonging to the second boy and away went that tie through the air too, blowing in the wind as Pink-Whistle carried it in his hand! He tied it high up in a bush.

"Here! What's happening?" cried the two boys, beginning to be scared. "Let's take the ship and go home!"

But now the invisible Mr Pink-Whistle was back again, and took the ship himself, right out of the hand of one of the big boys! He walked over to the boy who owned it, and put it into his hand. It looked exactly as if the boat had flown by itself through the air to its owner!

The two boys began to run but Mr Pink-Whistle ran too. He caught each of them by their collars, and down they went with a bump. One of them burst into tears. As the boy sat there Pink-Whistle undid his shoes and slid them off and to everyone's amazement, the shoes appeared to trot through the air all by themselves! "My shoes!" yelled the boy. "Look, my shoes!"

Somebody snatched at the shoes as they travelled through the air, held by the invisible Mr Pink-Whistle, and threw the into the pond – *splash-splash*! They sank at once.

"Oh good! That's what those boys did to my doll!" cried the girl with the pram. Everyone began to laugh. They pointed at the two boys, who had now got up from the ground. "It serves you right, it serves you right!" they cried.

One of the big boys lost his temper and rushed at a boy playing with a ball.

He kicked it right out of his hands and it rose in the air and went into a tree. It stayed there, caught in a branch.

"That's my new ball!" yelled the little boy.

"He'll get it for you!" cried a voice that seemed to come from nowhere. "Go on, you big bully, climb the tree and get the ball!" And the invisible Mr Pink-Whistle ran the big boy to the tree, caught hold of him by his trousers and jerked him up. He pushed him and prodded him, and

the boy, yelling with fright, found himself forced to climb up and get the ball.

It bounced down and the big boy began to climb down himself – but what was this? A circle of angry children closed round the bottom of the tree and a boy with a bat raised it high.

"What a chance to give him back some of the biffs he gave us!" he cried. "Come on, bully, climb down – see what will happen to you then!

The big boy yelled to his friend, "Come and help me, come on!" But his friend was no longer there! He had run off at top speed, scared at all these strange happenings.

The first boy climbed back into the tree again and sat there shivering with fright, looking down at the children waiting for him. Was all this a horrible dream?

A little whisper went round. "I say – can it be Mr Pink-Whistle doing all this? You know, it might be!"

Ooooh! Mr Pink-Whistle! The children stared at one another and then looked all round. But they couldn't see him, of course. "Please, please, if you're here, let us see you!" cried the little girl with the pram. "We know all about you!"

Mr Pink-Whistle was pleased. Now, how did they all know about him? He muttered the magic words that made him become visible again and the watching children saw a shadow first of all, and then a shape and then Mr Pink-Whistle himself, smiling all over his face! They crowded round him in joy.

"You always put things right, don't

171

you! Oh, Mr Pink-Whistle, we never thought you'd be here this morning! You did give those boys a fright!"

Mr Pink-Whistle saw an ice-cream man coming along and called to him. "Ice creams for everyone, please," he said.

The boy up the tree sat listening in amazement. Yes, he had heard of Mr Pink-Whistle too. Goodness – to think he had been behaving so badly when the little man came by! He felt ashamed and afraid. He began to slide quietly down the tree, hoping to creep away unseen and go home. But he suddenly saw something at the bottom of the tree and stopped.

It was a dog! Had Mr Pink-Whistle put it there to wait for him and bite him? The boy clambered back again at top speed, and looked longingly at the big ice creams.

Pink-Whistle hadn't put a dog there, of course. One of the small boys had placed his toy dog there while he went to eat his ice cream and, would you believe it, he forgot all about it and left it there at

the foot of the tree! Soon all the children went with Mr Pink-Whistle to the bus stop, and the scared boy up the tree was left alone, guarded by a toy dog! And there he stayed until the park-keeper came along and found him.

"Goodbye," said Mr Pink-Whistle to the delighted children as he climbed into the bus. "Don't worry about those boys any more. Just say 'Now where's Mr Pink-Whistle?' if you have any trouble and they'll run like the wind! Goodbye!"

Please Help Me, Mr Pink-Whistle

Mr Pink-Whistle, sir," said Sooty the cat, coming into the room where Mr Pink-Whistle was having a little snooze. "Could you wake up for a minute?"

"Hello! Dear me, was I asleep?" said Pink-Whistle, waking with a jump. "What is it, Sooty? A visitor to see me?"

"Well, it's a little boy," said Sooty, "and he seems to want your help – but he's so shy that really I can't make head or tail of what he wants!"

"Send him in," said Pink-Whistle, and Sooty ran out of the room and went to the front gate. A boy of about nine was there, looking anxiously at the house.

"You can come in," said Sooty. "And do try to speak properly or you will waste my master's time!"

The boy followed Sooty into the little house and blushed bright red with delight when he saw old Pink-Whistle, with pointed ears, green eyes and a very big smile.

"Hello, my boy," said Pink-Whistle. "What's the matter? I hear you want my help."

The boy nodded his head but didn't say a word. "Sit down," said Mr Pink-Whistle. 'Now tell me."

"P-p-p-p-please h-h-h-help m-m-m-m-m-m-m-me," said the boy, stammering dreadfully.

"I will," said Pink-Whistle. "What's wrong?"

"It's – it's – it's my st-st-stammer!" said the boy nervously. "I c-c-c-can't help it. And the others l-l-l-laugh at m-m-m-me and that m-m-m-akes it worse. and my m-m-m-mother gets c-c-cross t-t-too.

"Bad luck!" said Pink-Whistle. "You don't need to be nervous with me, you know. You will be glad to hear that I can cure you quite easily."

"C-c-can you?" said the boy, quite amazed.

"What's your name?" said Mr Pink-Whistle, "and your address? I'm going to send you something that will cure you."

The boy beamed all over his face. "My name's M-m-m-mark B-b-brown," he said.

"Not a good name for a stammerer," said Pink-Whistle, and twinkled at the boy. "I told you you don't need to be nervous with me. Take a deep breath and say your name again, slowly."

"Mark Brown!" said the boy. "What

are you g-going to send me, Mr Pink-Whistle?"

"Aha! Something alive!" said Pink-Whistle, shutting up the notebook in which he had written Mark's name and address. "Something that will want to understand every word you say. Something that will never laugh at you. Something that will want you to talk and talk so clearly that he is never at a loss to obey your smallest word."

"Is it something magic?" asked Mark, not stammering at all in his wonder at what Mr Pink-Whistle was saying.

"You wait and see," said Pink-Whistle. "Now, off you go, and I want you to visit me again in one month's time and bring my present back with you, so that I can see if you get along with it all right."

Mark ran off, puzzled and delighted. What did Mr Pink-Whistle mean? What a kind man he was – those twinkling eyes, that deep, happy voice! Yes, he felt sure that Mr Pink-Whistle would cure him of his stammering without any scolding or jeering, without any long, long exercises in speaking. Good old Mr Pink-Whistle!

Mr Pink-Whistle got busy as soon as Mark had gone. He went to his telephone and rang up Mark's mother. She was most astonished to hear who it was, and even more astonished when she knew that Mark had been to see him.

"It's his stammer he's worried about," said Mr Pink-Whistle. "I can cure it – if you will allow me to give him a present."

He told her what the present would be, and she said yes, she would let Mark have it as soon as it arrived, though for the life of her she couldn't see how it would help Mark's stammer!

Then Mr Pink-Whistle went off to the nearby farm and asked to see the little spaniel puppies that Floppy the lovely golden spaniel had in her basket. How pretty they were – and how they squirmed about, giving tiny little yaps all the time. Pink-Whistle longed to buy one for himself, but he knew that Sooty wouldn't like that at all. He chose a fat little puppy, with a silky golden coat, ears that drooped beautifully, and eyes that would melt anyone's heart!

Than night he took the puppy to Mark's home and gave it to Mark's mother. She had a little round basket all ready for it, with a warm rug inside. She was very grateful to Mr Pink-Whistle, and looked curiously at his pointed ears under his top hat. What a strange little man – and what a kind face.

"This puppy won't cure Mark's stammer, you know," she said. 'It's very kind of you to give it to him but I'm afraid not even you can cure Mark. We've all tried and failed."

"Never mind. Just give it to Mark," said Mr Pink-Whistle. "And tell him the puppy's name is Bonny."

"Oh dear he'll never say that!" said Mrs Brown. "B for Bonny is one of his worst stammering letters."

"The puppy's name is Bonny," said Mr Pink-Whistle firmly. "And it is on no account to be altered. Tell Mark he must train her properly, or else, at the end of a month, I shall take the puppy back. He must teach him what quite a lot of commands mean: Sit! Heel! Lie down! Quiet! and Down, girl, down! I shall expect Bonny to obey all those commands in a month's time. Please give Mark this note for me."

"Oh dear, he really won't be able to say a single command without stammering," said Mrs Brown. "It's no use, you know."

Mr Pink-Whistle raised his hat, said goodbye and went. How he wondered what Mark would say when he saw the puppy!

Later on Mark's mother crept upstairs with Bonny in the basket. The little thing wastired and was now fast asleep.

She set the basket down gently in Mark's room and went out. The boy was fast asleep, too, and didn't stir at all.

Bonny slept peacefully – but she awoke in the middle of the night and wanted her mother. Where was she? She couldn't feel her or smell her. She was very, very lonely indeed. She sat up in the basket, frightened, and began to whine.

Mark woke up at once, and he, too, sat up – what could that noise be? He listened in astonishment. It sounded like the whining of a dog!

He switched on his light and at once saw the tiny golden spaniel sitting forlornly in her basket, crying for his mother.

"Oh!" cried Mark. "It's a dream! Surely I'm dreaming!" He leaped out of bed and went over to the puppy. The little thing cuddled up to him, still whining. Then Mark saw a big white envelope in the basket and picked it up.

On the envelope was written: *From Mr Pink-Whistle to Mark*. Mark tore it open.

Here is the cure for your stammer, Mark, said the note. *Be sure Bonny understands every word you say. She doesn't even know what stammering is! Teach her all the things she ought to know. Your mother will tell you what I said. Love from Pink-Whistle*

Mark put the note down and stared at the tiny puppy. He cuddled it in his arms, and put his chin down on its soft head. "Bonny!" he said softly. "Yes, you're Bonny – it's a good name for you. So this is Mr Pink-Whistle's gift."

The puppy whined and cuddled closer. She liked this boy. He was warm and friendly and kind – the kind of boy that all dogs liked.

"I can't let you sleep alone in your basket the very first night!" said Mark. "I'll take you to bed with me, Bonny, and hope that Mum won't be cross – it'll only be just this once."

He cuddled the puppy again, loving its silky fur and beautiful ears. "I haven't stammered once to you, have I?" he said. "You wouldn't mind if I did – but it would puzzle you if I called you B-b-b-b-bonny, wouldn't it? It might even frighten you. You'll never laugh at me or be angry with me; you'll be my friend. And I shall be yours. If only I could tell Mr Pink-Whistle how happy I am!"

Mark was so happy next day that he hardly knew how to stop singing and

whistling. Bonny followed him about like a shadow. Everyone in the house loved the tiny creature, especially Janie, Mark's tomboy sister.

"Let me hold her, Mark, do let me!" she said.

"No-n-n-no," said Mark, with his usual stammer.

"There! You're stammering!" said Janie. "And yet you don't stammer when you talk to Bonny. You *can* help it, you see."

"I c-c-can't when I t-t-talk to p-p-people

like you, who l-l-laugh at me so often,"
said Mark. "I'm not afraid that B-bonny
will laugh."

"Listen, Mark, let me hold Bonny
sometimes and I promise, word of
honour, I won't laugh at you again," said
Janie. "Or mimic you. Not ever."

"All right. That'll b-be a help," said
Mark. "Bonny – here's my sister. She'll
love you, too!"

It certainly was a most extraordinary
thing, but whenever Mark spoke to
Bonny he never once stammered. He
soon began to teach the little thing how
to behave. At first Mark was sure he
would not be able to say "Down, girl,
down" without stammering over the D,
but it never bothered him at all. Mr Pink-
Whistle was right as usual!

Mark remembered that Mr Pink-
Whistle had told him to be sure to talk
and talk and talk to Bonny, so that she
would soon understand every word that
her little master said to her. So as soon as
he came home from school, Mark went to

fetch Bonny, took her to his room and played with her, and talked all the time.

He told Bonny all that happened at school. He showed her how to play ball and talked to her all about it. He told her over and over again of his visit to Mr Pink-Whistle.

His mother heard all the talking going on one day and popped her head in to listen. How amazed she was! Why, Mark didn't stammer once – not once. But when he saw her looking in, he stammered immediately he spoke to her. "Oh, M-m-mum, you made me j-jump!"

"Sorry," said his mother. "Oh, Mark – I've been listening to you talking to Bonny; you didn't stammer at all then,"

"I know," said Mark. "She wouldn't mind my stammering, but it might muddle her a bit – and besides, I don't even think about stammering when I'm with her. She's my friend. I know she won't laugh or jeer, so I don't have to think before I speak and then get afraid and stammer. She's curing me, Mum!"

"Yes, She is," said Mrs Brown. "Mr Pink-Whistle was right. Go on chattering to Bonny, Mark, you'll soon be so used to talking without a stammer that you won't even be afraid of stammering when you talk to people!"

At the end of the month Mark was sure he was cured. He had talked so much to Bonny, had taught her so many commands, and had quite forgotten to be afraid and nervous. Now he talked just as Janie did – fast and confidently without a single stammer.

"It's a miracle!" said Mrs Brown.

"No. Just common sense," said Mark's father. "I'd like to meet this Mr Pink-Whistle!"

But Mark went alone to see the kind little man, taking Bonny with him. The puppy already knew how to walk to heel, and was as good as gold.

"Hello. Nice to see you again!" said Mr Pink-Whistle. "Well, did the cure

I sent you work all right?" "Oh yes! I never stammer now!" said Mark. "Do you want to see how well I've trained Bonny?"

"Dear me, yes – if she's not been properly taught, I must have her back," said Pink-Whistle.

Then Mark gave all kinds of commands to little Bonny. "Sit! Lie down! Bark! Quiet now! Heel, girl, heel! On guard!"

Mr Pink-Whistle watched and listened. He felt very, very pleased. Mark turned to him with a flushed face and shining eyes. "There, Mr Pink-Whistle!" he said. "I can keep her, can't I? I love Bonny, she's my friend and I'm hers. She's cured me, just as you said she would."

"Well done, Mark!" said Mr Pink-Whistle. "Of course you can keep her, you deserve to have her – and she deserves to have you. Share her with Janie sometimes."

"I will," said Mark. "She helped me, too, because she never once laughed at me after I let her hold Bonny whenever she wanted to. I'm cured, aren't I?"

"You certainly are. You're quite a chatterbox now!" said Mr Pink-Whistle. "Let yourself out, will you – Sooty doesn't like puppies, I'm afraid."

"Goodbye, Mr Pink-Whistle, and thank you very much!" said Mark. "I'm going to tell everyone how to cure a stammer – just get a puppy to talk to!"

Well – it certainly does seem a very good idea, doesn't it?

Star Reads
Series 3

Enid Blyton

Magical and mischievous tales from Fairyland and beyond...

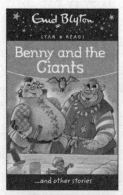

978-0-75372-654-9

978-0-75372-655-6

978-0-75372-656-3

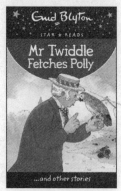

978-0-75372-657-0

978-0-75372-658-7

978-0-75372-659-4